Samuel French Acting Edition

Blast Radius

Part Two of
The Honeycomb Trilogy

by Mac Rogers

SAMUELFRENCH.COM   SAMUELFRENCH.CO.UK

MUSIC USE NOTE

Licensees are solely responsible for obtaining formal written permission from copyright owners to use copyrighted music in the performance of this play and are strongly cautioned to do so. If no such permission is obtained by the licensee, then the licensee must use only original music that the licensee owns and controls. Licensees are solely responsible and liable for all music clearances and shall indemnify the copyright owners of the play(s) and their licensing agent, Samuel French, against any costs, expenses, losses and liabilities arising from the use of music by licensees. Please contact the appropriate music licensing authority in your territory for the rights to any incidental music.

IMPORTANT BILLING AND CREDIT REQUIREMENTS

If you have obtained performance rights to this title, please refer to your licensing agreement for important billing and credit requirements.

THE HONEYCOMB TRILOGY was originally presented by Gideon Productions in three separate productions over the first half of 2012 at The Secret Theatre in Long Island City, New York. *ADVANCE MAN* ran in January 2012, *BLAST RADIUS* in March and April 2012, and *SOVEREIGN* in June 2012. The performances were directed by Jordana Williams and produced by Sean Willams and Shaun Bennet Fauntleroy, with sets by Sandy Yaklin, costumes by Amanda Jenks, lights by Jennifer Wilcox, sound by Jeanne Travis, props and effects by Stephanie Cox-Williams, fight choreography by Joseph Mathers, alien leg design by Zoe Morsotte, and publicity by Emily Owens PR. The Production Stage Manager was Devan Hibbard. The cast was as follows:

RONNIE	Becky Byers
ABBIE	David Rosenblatt
CONOR	Jason Howard
AMELIA	Kristen Vaughan
SHIRLEY	Nancy Sirianni
PECK	Adam Swiderski
CLEM	Alisha Spielmann
FEE	Felicia J. Hudson
JIMMY	Joe Mathers
DEV	Seth Shelden
WILLA	Cotton Wright
TASH	Amy Lee Pearsall

THE HONEYCOMB TRILOGY was subsequently presented by Gideon Productions in repertory at the Gym At Judson in New York City in October and November of 2015. The performances were directed by Jordana Williams and produced by Sean Williams, Rebecca Comtois, and Mikell Kober, with sets by Sandy Yaklin, costumes by Amanda Jenks, lights by Jennifer Wilcox, sound by Jeanne Travis, blood effects by Stephanie Cox-Williams, alien leg design by Zoe Morsotte and Lauren Genutis, fight choreography by Adam Swiderski, and publicity by Emily Owens PR. The Production Stage Manager was Devan Hibbard and the Assistant Director was Mikell Kober.

RONNIE	Becky Byers
ABBIE	David Rosenblatt
CONOR	Jason Howard
AMELIA	Kristen Vaughan
SHIRLEY	Nancy Sirianni
PECK	Adam Swiderski
CLEM	Alisha Spielmann
FEE	Felicia J. Hudson

JIMMY	Joe Mathers
DEV	Seth Shelden
WILLA	Cotton Wright
TASH	Amy Lee Pearsall

CHARACTERS

The Cooke family members can be any race/ethnicity. It would probably work best if they look biologically related.

RONNIE COOKE – 30, female
ABBIE COOKE – 27, male
AMELIA COOKE – 50s, female
CONOR – 50s, male, any ethnicity
PECK – 20s to 40s, male, any ethnicity
SHIRLEY – late 50s to early 60s, female, any ethnicity
CLEM – 20s, female, any ethnicity
FEE – 20s, female, any ethnicity
JIMMY – 20s, male, any ethnicity
DEV – 20s, male, any ethnicity
WILLA – 20s or 30s, female, any ethnicity
TASH – 20s to 30s, female, any ethnicity

SETTING

The Cooke family's living room twelve years after the events of *Advance Man*.

ACT ONE

One

(Twelve years after the events of Advance Man.)

(The living room of the former Cooke household. Night, lit only by oil lanterns. The living room is now with cracks, weathering, and mold showing. It's not filthy, though. Some of the old furniture – including the sofa – remain, but in a dilapidated state.)

(The front door has been crudely altered to be much larger. There are several pairs of muddy boots by the door. Outside the windows is the mangrove-dominated vegetation found in swamps, mixed with startling extraterrestrial plant life.)

*(**SHIRLEY**, **FEE**, and **CLEM** surround a heavily pregnant woman, **TASH**, who is lying on a cot with her belly exposed and a root of some kind in her mouth. Another unused cot lies nearby. **SHIRLEY**'s older than the others. **FEE** and **CLEM** are noticeably pregnant. **RONNIE** looks out a window. A number of weapon-like gardening implements, reapers, hang on the wall.)*

SHIRLEY. Do you feel it?

FEE. I don't know.

SHIRLEY. You don't know? Feel it. Dig your hands in.

FEE. I can't.

SHIRLEY. You can. She needs you to. Get your hands in there. Ronnie!

RONNIE. In a minute.

SHIRLEY. Now. She's losing the choopie stick. That's your job. *(to* **FEE***)* Dig your hands in.

CLEM. Let me.

> *(She pushes her hands into* **TASH***'s belly.* **TASH** *cries out.)*

Sorry, sorry Tash!

> *(***RONNIE** *puts the root in* **TASH***'s mouth. She clamps down on it.)*

SHIRLEY. *(to* **FEE***)* Now you.

FEE. It hurts her!

SHIRLEY. Hurt her a lot more to leave it like this.

> *(***SHIRLEY** *catches* **RONNIE** *craning her neck to look out the window.)*

Ronnie! Eyes here! Both of you: you need to know how to do this. Get your hands in there.

> *(***RONNIE** *presses into* **TASH***'s belly.* **TASH** *groans.)*

Feel it?

RONNIE. Yeah.

SHIRLEY. Baby's crossways, right? Baby's breech. No way it's coming out, kill both of them. Old days, Time Before, we would've cut, but we don't have the stuff to do that safely now. This is our only shot. It's still small enough, maybe we can turn it and it'll come out breathing. You watch what I do, you watch how I do it. You're gonna see more of these, you need to know.

> *(***SHIRLEY** *presses her hands into* **TASH***'s belly, carefully turning the baby in increments.* **TASH** *wails into the root.)*

FEE. You're killing her!

SHIRLEY. Hey! Everyone! What do we need?

FEE, CLEM, RONNIE. *(not in unison)* Every baby.

SHIRLEY. What do we need?!

FEE, CLEM, RONNIE. *(in unison)* Every baby!

(In the distance, a thunderous explosion. All stop and stare. **RONNIE** *leaps to her feet and runs to a window.)*

SHIRLEY. All right, that's for later. We're on this. Ronnie!

RONNIE. Peck's that way!

SHIRLEY. And you running out there does what? For him or anyone? You're doing *this* now.

CLEM. It's turning! Oh shit, it's turning!

SHIRLEY. All right, let me work alone.

RONNIE. *(scanning the sky)* Flyer's coming!

SHIRLEY. 'Course a flyer's coming. Bomb went off, your brother's gonna wanna throw weight around.

RONNIE. Abbie's back?

CLEM. Shirley it's turned!

SHIRLEY. Quiet now.

CLEM. I can't believe it!

FEE. She's gonna bite clean through!

CLEM. Did we save the baby?

SHIRLEY. Won't know until.

RONNIE. Who the fuck has bombs? How?

CLEM. Shirley, that was like magic.

SHIRLEY. Might be nothing. We'll see.

RONNIE. Coming down now! *(She grabs a reaper off the wall.)* Two on its back, my brother and Skin.

SHIRLEY. Lose the reaper.

RONNIE. And they're carrying something. Can't tell what.

SHIRLEY. Hey! You can't have a reaper when they come in!

(The sound of huge insect legs skittering across the roof and down the side of the house.)

RONNIE. *(looking out the window)* It's a person.

SHIRLEY. What is?

RONNIE. What they're carrying. It's a person.

CONOR. *(offstage)* House Four! May I be admitted?

RONNIE. Identify yourself!

CONOR. *(offstage)* Conor Honeycomb!

RONNIE. I thought bugs didn't have names.

SHIRLEY. Ronnie, open the door!

> **(RONNIE** *heaves the door open.* **CONOR** *enters, carrying an unconscious young woman.)*

CONOR. Where can I put her?

RONNIE. Who is she?

CONOR. She was hurt in the blast, please. She's carrying.

CLEM. *(to* **SHIRLEY***)* It's Willa House Ten.

CONOR. She's carrying, she needs to be here, Ronnie, please.

SHIRLEY. Don't talk to Ronnie, talk to *me.*

RONNIE. *(to* **CLEM***)* She told you she was carrying?

CLEM. Everybody's carrying, I don't remember.

CONOR. She reported missing her menstrual cycle, she told many others. Where may I put her please?

ABBIE. *(entering)* The other cot, Ambassador, and you don't have to ask permission.

> **(ABBIE** *and* **RONNIE** *look at each other.* **CONOR** *hurries over to the cot and sets* **WILLA** *down carefully.)*

SHIRLEY. What happened to her?

ABBIE. *(moving toward* **SHIRLEY***)* What, you didn't hear the explosion?

> **(RONNIE** *steps into his path, reaper raised.)*

RONNIE. That's close enough.

ABBIE. Shirley?

RONNIE. We have a right to protect our house and our babies.

ABBIE. Shirley House Four, are you allowing this?

SHIRLEY. Ronnie, put that in Clem's hands or you leave this house tonight.

CLEM. Come on. This is stupid.

(**RONNIE** *hands over the reaper.* **SHIRLEY** *goes to*
WILLA.)

SHIRLEY. Hit her head?

CONOR. That's correct, she struck it rather hard during
the explosion.

(**SHIRLEY** *examines her.*)

ABBIE. Interesting, isn't it? Fourth bomb in a month.

RONNIE. You know who's doing it?

ABBIE. Do you?

RONNIE. Any dead?

CONOR. Eric House Fifteen, Sandra House Sixteen, Mick
House Twenty-One.

CLEM. Fuck.

FEE. Mick came by just today. Delivery.

ABBIE. And now he never will again. You might want to pass
that on to anyone involved in this. You might wanna
let them know they're mostly killing other humans. A
bomb might kill one of the Honeycomb, more likely
injure, but it'll definitely kill four or five of you. You
might want to ask them what's the point.

RONNIE. Since when are you delivering injured personally?

ABBIE. I'm not. I came to see Mom.

SHIRLEY. *(to* **CONOR***)* She's gonna live. Can't tell about the
baby. On the brain front, I'm just gonna have to wait
for her to wake up.

RONNIE. Remember how they used to have machines for
that? For looking at people's heads?

SHIRLEY. All right, Ronnie.

RONNIE. CAT scans? Am I right?

CLEM. MRI…?

RONNIE. MRI, right! What did that stand for? "Mental"
something?

SHIRLEY. Ronnie, that's enough.

CONOR. Magnetic Resonance Imaging.

*(**RONNIE** looks at **CONOR**.)*

RONNIE. See, that's interesting.

ABBIE. *(to **SHIRLEY**)* Everyone in bed. Now.

> *(**SHIRLEY** nods to **CLEM** and **FEE**, who exit up the stairs. To **RONNIE**:)*

You too.

RONNIE. Nice trip? Got back fast.

CONOR. Just to the Pacific Northwest this time. We don't have to cross the ocean until next season.

RONNIE. Is that where they made you that Nampas outfit?

ABBIE. Get used to it. We'll be wearing them here, too.

RONNIE. The slaves dying out there as fast as they do here?

ABBIE. *(to **SHIRLEY**, meaning **RONNIE**)* Why is this still happening?

SHIRLEY. Ronnie: upstairs. Now.

RONNIE. *(leaving, to **SHIRLEY**)* Don't give them anything, don't concede *anything*.

CONOR. I'm happy to see you, Ronnie.

RONNIE. Now that you're back, *Ambassador*, maybe you can do something about the smell. Maybe get your people to quit shitting in the woods. Something to think about.

SHIRLEY. Now!

> *(**RONNIE** exits.)*

ABBIE. Can you control her or not?

SHIRLEY. I'm sorry, Ambassadors.

ABBIE. Her baby's weaned. She leaves tomorrow.

SHIRLEY. That's understood, Ambassador.

CONOR. *(looking at **ABBIE**)* We're satisfied, Shirley House Four.

SHIRLEY. *(meaning **TASH** and **WILLA**)* I gotta get back to these.

CONOR. May I assist you?

SHIRLEY. Assist me?

CONOR. And perhaps speak with you concurrently?

SHIRLEY. Concurrently. Sure. I think I remember that one.

> (**CONOR** *kneels down with* **SHIRLEY** *as she examines* **WILLA** *and* **TASH**.)

Only so much I can do. This one, you should've kept her awake. She may never wake up again. Start any time you want.

CONOR. The Honeycomb has decided against reprisals.

SHIRLEY. Oh yeah?

CONOR. At my urging, the Honeycomb has chosen not to impose greater restrictions on Coral Farm in response to the attacks.

SHIRLEY. That's appreciated.

ABBIE. That can change. Keep blowing things up, anything can change.

SHIRLEY. Who am I talking to here?

CONOR. We know human bodies get tired faster than Honeycomb bodies.

SHIRLEY. Well, you've got one.

CONOR. If the explosions were to stop, if they were to cease for a reasonable period of time –

ABBIE. I can't goddam believe it!

SHIRLEY. Who says we have anything to do with it?

CONOR. Perhaps you don't. But should you have any knowledge whatsoever, any influence with any relevant parties, even any information that will assist us in solving this problem… The Honeycomb is prepared to reduce the farming day by a quarter.

ABBIE. Shameful.

SHIRLEY. The whole farm, the whole camp, every house? A quarter off?

> (**AMELIA** *appears at the top of the stairs. She's clearly ill.*)

ABBIE. Please, don't pause to thank us for either of the two previous reductions.

CONOR. You have my word, you have the word of the Honeycomb.

AMELIA. Abbie?

> *(All turn to her.)*

Abbie, oh my god.

ABBIE. Yeah, Mom.

AMELIA. Oh, I didn't know you were back! *(She goes to him, embraces him.)*

SHIRLEY. *(to* **CONOR***)* I'll look into it.

CONOR. Thank you.

AMELIA. I would have cleaned.

ABBIE. Cleaned?

AMELIA. Look at you, you're sunburned. You have to be careful.

SHIRLEY. Why doesn't Abbie come see you up in your room, Amelia?

AMELIA. Where were you?

ABBIE. Just on a trip, Northwest, not far.

AMELIA. Northwest?

ABBIE. We got a lot of good work done, a lot of training, a lot of –

AMELIA. No one tried to hurt you?

ABBIE. Who would try to hurt me?

CONOR. Amelia.

> *(***AMELIA*** stiffens and looks at* ***CONOR***.)*

AMELIA. Ambassador.

CONOR. Are you...at all...improved?

AMELIA. Improved?

> *(A strange sound, like unearthly cicadas, comes from outside the unseen downstage windows.* ***AMELIA*** *winces.)*

CONOR. It's all right, Amelia, it's all right, you don't have to be frightened.

AMELIA. Ask them to stop, please.

CONOR. They're singing to you.

AMELIA. Tell them to stop.

CONOR. They're paying tribute. You're the First Ambassador.

ABBIE. Jesus Christ, Mom, it's a good thing.

AMELIA. *(barely holding it together)* Please, please tell them to stop.

ABBIE. *(to* **CONOR***)* We're staying the night, anyway.

> *(Over the following,* **ABBIE** *goes to the window and signals to the creatures outside using hand gestures that resemble sign language. The sounds diminish and cease, and we hear one insect walk up the wall of the house and fly away.)*

SHIRLEY. Maybe Abbie can come see you up in your room.

AMELIA. All right.

SHIRLEY. Just lie down and you can talk and that'll be easier for you, right?

CONOR. *(to* **ABBIE***)* Your fluency with the hands language. Better than I am, I think.

ABBIE. In a generation this will be the only language. It's ridiculous that everyone doesn't know it already.

SHIRLEY. Ambassadors, would you like to join us?

AMELIA. *(to* **ABBIE***)* I'm sorry it looks like this.

ABBIE. Everything is great, Mom. Everything's perfect.

> *(He and* **SHIRLEY** *gently guide* **AMELIA** *up the stairs.)*

Conor.

CONOR. A moment.

> *He goes to* **WILLA** *and looks at her. At that moment,* **PECK** *nearly enters from the kitchen and walks directly into their sight. He meets eyes with* **SHIRLEY** *and backs out quickly and quietly with no one else seeing him.)*

AMELIA. Did you see Ronnie?

ABBIE. Yeah, Mom, I did.

AMELIA. You did? Did you talk to her?

ABBIE. I saw Ronnie, Mom, I promise.

> (**ABBIE**, **AMELIA**, *and* **SHIRLEY** *exit, followed by* **CONOR**. **PECK** *creeps back into the room.* **WILLA** *gasps and opens her eyes.* **PECK** *freezes, waits to see if she'll cry out.* **WILLA** *lies back down, closes her eyes.* **PECK** *starts to leave.* **RONNIE** *runs down the stairs.*)

RONNIE. Mother. Fucker. *(She runs into his arms.)*

PECK. I'm good, I was nowhere near. But Eric, he's –

RONNIE. Shut the fuck up.

> *(They kiss, intensely.)*

Tell me.

PECK. Like he swallowed a bomb. Like he blew up from the inside.

RONNIE. What the fuck?

PECK. Might be them.

RONNIE. Except they think it's us.

PECK. I'll get going.

RONNIE. Like hell you will.

> (**RONNIE** *kisses him. It gets more intense.*)

PECK. This soon?

RONNIE. Soon? It's been *months*. I hate the babies.

PECK. No you don't.

RONNIE. I hand them right over. I only like fucking and I only like fucking *you*. But you know what?

PECK. You need another one.

> *(He picks her up. She wraps her legs around him.)*

RONNIE. You're goddamn right I need another one.

PECK. I'll give you one.

RONNIE. Yeah?

PECK. Sure.

RONNIE. You'll give me a baby? You fucker, you'll give me a baby?

PECK. Come on.

> *(He carries her out to the kitchen.)*

Two

(Dawn. **CONOR** *sits by* **WILLA**, *reading a book.*
ABBIE *comes downstairs.)*

CONOR. Did you sleep?

ABBIE. Sort of.

CONOR. And Amelia?

> *(***ABBIE*** gestures: it's bad. Beat.)*

May I read something to you?

ABBIE. You shouldn't have that.

CONOR. The young man Douglas goes to the girl Anna's
father. The father is Peterson. He owns a great deal of
property.

ABBIE. What book is that?

> *(***CONOR*** holds up the book cover so* **ABBIE** *can
> see.)*

CONOR. Peterson won't let Anna marry Douglas. Douglas
owns very little property.

ABBIE. God, look at that.

CONOR. Douglas goes to Peterson, listen to this:

ABBIE. Conor, you realize –

CONOR. "It's true that I'm a poor boy. It's true that
I have nothing to offer your Anna but a room above
my workshop. But I ask you, sir, to consider this: My
position is one of great responsibility. I make saddles
for generals and queens. If you speak to any of the
men who fought by me in the war gone by, any one of
them will tell you that I am brave and reliable under
fire. I have forged the strength of my character in both
commerce and blood, and I offer that strength to your
daughter for both our lifetimes."

ABBIE. You know that's garbage, right?

CONOR. Garbage?

ABBIE. If you're going to break Law, you should risk it for
better books.

CONOR. You had better books than this?

ABBIE. Conor...yes, we had better books than this.

CONOR. Because this is entrancing. Do you know that Peterson still says no? After those words? And because the young man owns less property!

ABBIE. Well, people aren't judged like that anymore. Thanks to you.

CONOR. People also aren't married anymore.

(**WILLA** *shivers violently.*)

ABBIE. Is she all right?

CONOR. She's cold.

(**CONOR** *sets down the book and caresses* **WILLA.**)

ABBIE. How could she be cold?

CONOR. She just woke up in a new body: soft, exposed, nerve endings multiplied a thousandfold. The million voices she's heard in her mind all her life have gone silent. There isn't an exact feeling to go with all that newness, so the mind tells her she's cold. *(beat)* Your mother's touch, on my face, my arms, like this...for many months it was my only relief.

ABBIE. I hate these bodies.

CONOR. That's not true, is it?

ABBIE. It is true.

CONOR. When I touch your body and you cry out, is that pain?

ABBIE. No, you're right.

CONOR. *(going to* **ABBIE***)* I concentrate absolutely when I touch you. I want to be perfect.

ABBIE. You are.

CONOR. Don't say you hate our bodies.

ABBIE. Think about something. Think about when I'm touching you all the way.

CONOR. Do you mean orgasm?

ABBIE. And we're very close together. And I'm watching
your face, and you're looking back at me, and there's
a feeling, in those moments, that we're as close as two
humans can be.

CONOR. Yes.

ABBIE. But then – just think, and be truthful – that last
moment before orgasm: isn't it true that at that
moment the closeness stops? Think about it. All your
attention is turned inside, and you have to move just
right, concentrating only on yourself in order to finish?

CONOR. Is that how it is?

ABBIE. That, right there, is everything you need to know
about human life. Extraordinary effort to achieve
split-seconds of connection before it's all lost in the
thrashing.

CONOR. I'll keep my eyes open.

ABBIE. Compare that to the Honeycomb. Where you
just live, always, inside each other's minds. *That's*
connection, that's perfect pleasure, it doesn't well up
like a blister 'til it pops, it just *is*, *always*.

CONOR. I'll keep my eyes on you the whole time. I didn't
know that's what you wanted.

ABBIE. Sometimes, when I've been in the Honeycomb
for weeks, I think I can hear it. Is there any way that's
possible?

CONOR. I don't know, Abbie.

ABBIE. Well…lie, then.

CONOR. *(going to* **ABBIE***)* I can't. Not to you. This love here,
yours for me, mine for you, this is a Honeycomb of our
very own. There are no lies in the Honeycomb.

> *(They kiss.* **ABBIE** *puts an arm around* **CONOR**
> *and looks at* **WILLA***.)*

ABBIE. This has to work.

CONOR. Maybe it doesn't. Shirley's reasonable.

ABBIE. It doesn't matter how reasonable she is, she can't control Ronnie. *(meaning* **WILLA***)* We need her moving, we need her verbal. We're running out of time.

CONOR. She's not like me. She's a soldier. And she's prepared.

ABBIE. It always amazes me how *fast* it is. Every time. Transferring a mind between bodies, how is it so fast?

CONOR. The process is nothing. Establish the telepathic connection, then sever it. *This* is the part that's hard. I wish I could have nursed her through this in the Honeycomb.

ABBIE. If she'd vanished for months and suddenly reappeared, they wouldn't let her through the door. It's better like this, the explosion gives us cover.

CONOR. The explosion.

ABBIE. How are they doing it? It's impossible, right?

CONOR. Someone's doing it. It can't be impossible.

ABBIE. *(looking up the stairs)* I have to get Ronnie out of this house. Someone's gonna kill her. One of us, one of hers, but someone's gonna kill her. And she'll deserve it.

> *(Sounds upstairs: the house is waking up.)*

The book. The book!

> **(CONOR** *conceals the book.* **SHIRLEY** *comes downstairs.)*

SHIRLEY. Ambassadors.

ABBIE. Shirley House Four.

SHIRLEY. Breakfast, or are you on your way?

ABBIE. I'm seeing Mom and then we're leaving. **(ABBIE** *exits upstairs.)*

CONOR. Shirley House Four, I wonder if I can ask you for a liberty?

> *(She looks at him.)*

May I help you look after her?

SHIRLEY. Are you serious?

CONOR. And come to visit her sometimes?

SHIRLEY. You're the one who gives the orders.

CONOR. The disorientation when we found her, the loss of language, the fear. It reminds me of my own injury.

SHIRLEY. Whatever you want.

CONOR. Thank you, Shirley House Four.

ABBIE. *(offstage)* Now!

> (**RONNIE** *appears as* **ABBIE** *shoves her onto the stairs.* **ABBIE** *appears just above her.*)

You're going back to work, right now. You're not staying here one more minute.

Three

(Afternoon. **FEE** *checks out the windows.* **CLEM** *reclines on the couch.* **WILLA** *sleeps on the cot.)*

CLEM. I need the pisser.

FEE. You know where it is.

CLEM. Who is it today?

FEE. Supposed to be just Peck, but I hear Ronnie too.

CLEM. Is she crazy? Peck they'll lash. Ronnie they'll kill.

FEE. Just what I heard.

CLEM. If I piss on this couch, you think Ronnie might sit in it by accident?

JIMMY. *(outside the door)* Fee!

FEE. Shit!

CLEM. Who is it? Nampas?

FEE. We have reapers, we're defended!

JIMMY. *(offstage)* Is that Fee?

FEE. Jimmy?

DEV. *(offstage)* Can you hold the door open?

CLEM. Oh god, it's both of them.

DEV. *(offstage)* Please?

CLEM. I'm seven months! You can't push?

DEV. *(offstage)* Not carrying this we can't!

> *(***FEE** *helps* **CLEM** *to hold the door open.* **JIMMY** *and* **DEV** *enter, each holding an end of an enormous, multiply-jointed insect leg that they drop on the couch.)*

JIMMY. Who's a big bug NOW?

CLEM. Shit, Jimmy!

DEV. Crazy, right?

JIMMY. *(to* **FEE***)* Got it for you, girl!

CLEM. Get it off there, are you crazy?

FEE. You pulled that off a dead bug?

JIMMY. Yeah, dead!

DEV. That's what we'll do next time, we'll pull one off a live bug. Go bigger.

CLEM. Guys! You can't have this here!

JIMMY. Man, fuck a leg, I'll pull off a 'tenna, I'll walk right up in a bug's face and be all like – *(He mimics wrenching the antenna off of a giant insect)* – "Mine now!"

CLEM. If they find that here they kill us all –

JIMMY. *(to* **FEE***)* And I'll give that to you too, girl.

FEE. You're so stupid. *(She kisses him.)*

CLEM. Dev!

DEV. *(to* **CLEM***)* All right, you're right.

CLEM. Get it out of here!

DEV. I will, I am. *(He picks up one end of the leg.)*

FEE. That's weird, you never see 'em dead.

CLEM. 'Cause they go to the Honeycomb to die, it's really important to them! If they see this it's like the worst thing you can do!

FEE. Where did you find it?

JIMMY. Oh, you're not getting it.

DEV. I'm moving it! Jimmy, can you –

JIMMY. We didn't *find* it dead. *(beat)*

CLEM. Are you off your mind?

JIMMY. That's *right*! Reaper up underneath, right between the first two legs.

DEV. Well, it was me first, really.

FEE. You are *lying*.

JIMMY. I'm not lying!

CLEM. Are you off your fucking mind?

DEV. Jimmy help with this.

JIMMY. Look in my eyes, girl. Truth.

DEV. It was off by itself. Way more north than they usually go.

CLEM. What were you doing there?

DEV. You know, just…

CLEM. Smoking choopie, right?

DEV. Look, a little bit.

JIMMY. Shit, a little bit for *you.*

DEV. You have to get a bit away from Settlement or they smell it, or whatever they do.

FEE. Why was it all the way up there?

JIMMY. Looking for Shirley's bombs, right? That's what I think.

FEE. Shirley doesn't have bombs.

JIMMY. Shirley's got *something.* Or Ronnie, I bet it's Ronnie.

DEV. Jimmy, come on, help me here.

JIMMY. *(to FEE)* Can I get in it?

FEE. What?

JIMMY. "What?" I said can I get in it?

FEE. Boy look at the size of me!

CLEM. Look, I'll do it. *(She moves to pick up the other side of the leg.)*

DEV. No, Clem, you can't. Come on. Jimmy!

JIMMY. *(to FEE.)* Put your legs up or whatever.

FEE. You're so stupid.

JIMMY. Well can I get something?

FEE. Something. Maybe.

DEV. Jimmy!

JIMMY. Maybe? I brought you this *leg.*

FEE. What am I gonna do with that leg?

DEV. Jimmy *now.*

JIMMY. Hold up, hold up – Dev. My brother.

DEV. Brother?

JIMMY. Can you do watch? Me and Fee need to do something. My *brother.*

DEV. All right, but right after, *right after*, you have to help me –

CLEM. No! No right after, right now. That is death, sitting right in this room!

JIMMY. Come on, Clem –

> (**PECK** *enters.*)

CLEM. Death for all of us! Even me, even Fee! Kill a bug, it doesn't matter if you're carrying! Get that out of here now!

PECK. Fuck is this?

> (*All fall silent.*)

The fuck. Is this.

JIMMY. Peck, Peck, my friend, my brother –

DEV. It's not Clem and Fee, they're not part of it.

PECK. Yeah. I guessed that.

JIMMY. Peck, my brother, it's all good, when I tell you how it happened – this was *defense.*

PECK. No it wasn't. Bug doesn't attack unless you attack first.

DEV. We were up by the north mangroves. Bug surprised us. We didn't know if we were outside Law or what, we didn't know what it would say to the Honeycomb. We just did it. Peck, they're never up there!

PECK. Except flyovers.

JIMMY. Exactly! My brother.

PECK. And things're blowing up. And nobody knows why. So that's when they're gonna do flyovers. Right?

> (*He seizes* **JIMMY**'*s face, looks in his eyes.*)

Fucking idiot.

JIMMY. Peck, man, my eyes are funny 'cause I'm sick, it's not what you think –

PECK. And your breath?

> (*He slaps* **JIMMY** *in the side of the head.*)

JIMMY. Peck, shit!

> (**PECK** *crosses to* **DEV**.)

DEV. Peck, look, you're right, I get it –

> (**PECK** *slaps him as well.*)

PECK. Where's the rest?

DEV. Of the choopie?

PECK. Of the *bug*.

JIMMY. We left it there, man, I swear!

DEV. We just brought the leg. I mean I know that doesn't make it right, but we just brought the leg back, I promise.

PECK. I believe you.

JIMMY. See? My man!

PECK. I *believe* you did an unauthorized kill, fuckin' up Shirley right in the middle of negotiating less time on the farm. I *believe* you just brought the leg, and left the whole rest of the bug in plain fucking sight, not digested in the Honeycomb like Law says, but rotting in the *fucking sun*! That right?

DEV. We'll go back.

PECK. Yep.

JIMMY. Peck, brother, I promise we'll go back, but can I just grab a minute –

DEV. We'll go back *right now*, and we'll find a place to hide it.

PECK. Not hide. Bury.

JIMMY. Man, *bury*?

PECK. Under a bunch of mangroves so you can't see it from the sky.

DEV. Dig? In the mangroves? Peck, the roots, man –

PECK. Yep.

JIMMY. That'll take all night! We're on detail tomorrow!

PECK. Probably won't do that again, then.

JIMMY. Man, fuck!

PECK. *(to FEE)* Shirley back yet?

FEE. Not sure when. I know she's expecting you. You hear Ronnie might be coming?

PECK. What?

FEE. Just what I heard.

PECK. *(to* **JIMMY** *and* **DEV***)* I'll be back in a minute. You'll be gone. *(He exits out the kitchen.)*

DEV. Come on.

JIMMY. *(pulling* **FEE** *towards a corner)* Just real quick, just real quick.

FEE. Are you crazy?

CLEM. You have to get that thing out of here!

FEE. You think I feel like it now?

JIMMY. Just real quick.

FEE. Oh, "just real quick."

CLEM. *(to* **DEV***)* Can you control him?

JIMMY. *(to* **FEE***)* I could die. Me and Dev, we could go out there and die.

DEV. I don't think we're gonna die –

CLEM. *(overlapping)* You could *always* die –

JIMMY. We could die, this could be it, we might never see each other again. I gotta feel you, girl. I gotta feel you next to me, I got to.

> *(***FEE*** relents. They move the rest of the way into the corner and start making out. After a while* **FEE** *starts jerking* **JIMMY** *off.)*

Keep a lookout, man!

DEV. Yeah.

> *(A beat between* **CLEM** *and* **DEV***.)*

So...how are you?

CLEM. Well, I want this leg gone.

DEV. Sure.

CLEM. What're you doing smoking choopie?

DEV. I'll stop, I won't do it anymore.

CLEM. Why were you doing it already? You never did it before.

DEV. You know...something to do.

> *(***CLEM*** gives him a look.)*

So I don't think about it.

CLEM. What?

DEV. You're here, and I'm not supposed to be here. You come out, it'll be the same: you'll be House Ten, I'll be across the marsh in Eighteen, they'll put the baby in House One with the other babies...

CLEM. So, we sneak around like everybody.

DEV. I miss you all the time. Like... I miss you all the time. But not when I smoke choopie.

CLEM. Well, shit. *(She kisses him.)* You're gonna be a pain to me with those eyes. Don't let the baby have those eyes.

> *(They kiss again.)*

DEV. What if I asked to join the Nampas?

CLEM. Dev.

DEV. We'd get special treatment.

CLEM. You just killed a bug, pulled its leg off, and now you wanna join the Nampas?

DEV. So it'd be easier for us. *(beat)*

CLEM. Here's what you do: Don't smoke the choopie.

DEV. I won't.

CLEM. No, listen to me: Don't smoke the choopie. Take the pain instead. Walk right into it, keep walking, walk right out of it. There's no choopie like how that feels. That's the best.

DEV. Then I will.

> **(FEE** *notices something out the window over* **JIMMY**'s *shoulder.)*

FEE. Oh shit they're back!

DEV. Shit shit!

JIMMY. Man I said watch!

CLEM. You gotta go!

JIMMY. *(finishing himself off and kissing her)* You're beautiful. You're beautiful, girl.

> *(He hurries over to where* **DEV** *already has the other end of the leg.)*

DEV. Jimmy!

JIMMY. Well come on, man!

DEV. *Me* come on?

JIMMY. *(indicating the blanket over* **WILLA***)* Gimme that blanket real quick!

CLEM. It's on a girl!

JIMMY. You want *her* to see?

> (**CLEM** *and* **FEE** *pull the blanket off* **WILLA** *and drape it over the leg.* **WILLA** *shivers, legs jerking in unison.)*

JIMMY. Whoa.

CLEM. Get out of here!

JIMMY. Bitch is *creepy*.

DEV. Let's go.

JIMMY. Okay, now open the door when I say.

DEV. *(to* **CLEM***)* Walk into it?

CLEM. And keep walking.

JIMMY. Now!

> (**FEE** *opens the door. As* **SHIRLEY** *and* **PECK** *step in,* **JIMMY** *and* **CLEM** *race past her with the covered leg.)*

JIMMY. Good to see you Shirley!

DEV. Good to see you Shirley! *(They race off into the night.)*

FEE. Sorry, Shirley.

SHIRLEY. This is supposed to be a secret meetup. Sounds like a goddam campfire night.

PECK. They won't be back tonight, trust me.

SHIRLEY. We gotta be ready to break any time. Abbie and Skin could be back *any time.*

> (*A sound from the kitchen. Everyone tenses;* **PECK** *grabs a reaper off the wall.)*

PECK. Expecting anybody?

SHIRLEY. No.

(**PECK** *approaches the kitchen door.*)

RONNIE. *(from the periphery)* All clear?

SHIRLEY. Ronnie?

PECK. All clear.

(*She runs in and kisses* **PECK**.)

CLEM. I need the pisser.

(*She exits out the front door.*)

SHIRLEY. Ronnie, you can't be here!

RONNIE. I heard there was a meetup.

SHIRLEY. You've got no reason to be in House One, and if your brother finds out you were –

RONNIE. Sure I do. *(She touches her stomach.)*

PECK. What?

RONNIE. *(to PECK)* Thanks to you. *(beat)*

SHIRLEY. You're not lying?

RONNIE. I've done this a couple of times. I know what to look for. Did you save my bed for me?

SHIRLEY. No, but you can sleep in a different one. Ronnie:

RONNIE. Yeah, I know.

SHIRLEY. No. You listen to me. I'm not gonna let you endanger this house. I'm not gonna let you wreck everything we've built. You're either here and walking the line or you're somewhere else.

(**TASH** *appears on the stairs.*)

RONNIE. Did you promise the bugs something you can't deliver or not?

TASH. Ronnie?

RONNIE. Tash. (**RONNIE** *walks over to her.*)

SHIRLEY. Hey there. Are you sure you're okay to be up?

RONNIE. Tash, I heard.

(**TASH** *comes downstairs and embraces* **RONNIE**.)

TASH. They just took her.

RONNIE. I know.

TASH. They just took her little body to the Honeycomb.

RONNIE. They take everybody.

SHIRLEY. Tash, we could've…you know in the old days we could've…

RONNIE. I'm kinda thinking about paying them back. What do you think?

TASH. I'll do anything.

RONNIE. Well, I'll tell you what, why don't you help us out with our little problem?

SHIRLEY. Hey, Ronnie? It's my meetup, I say what we're talking about, and in what order.

RONNIE. So let's *not* talk about the explosions yet, let's talk about the more *urgent* stuff first. *(beat)*

SHIRLEY. Who has eyewitnesses?

FEE. Jesse House Seven came by with veggies. She was at the east fleshies, talked to some other folks there.

SHIRLEY. Anything?

FEE. Not really. Everybody there was supposed to be there, everybody worked all night right up until.

RONNIE. What about the Nampas?

FEE. Nobody saw anything funny. The same five bugs, the same twelve Nampas, and nobody saw them move all night.

RONNIE. What the *hell*?

> *(Over the following,* **CLEM** *returns and heads for the stairs.)*

SHIRLEY. Maybe they snuck down from Cubano. Not bugs, but some Nampas, if they were quiet –

RONNIE. Let's stick to what we know, not what we guess.

SHIRLEY. Excuse me?

RONNIE. *(to CLEM)* Hang out a second.

CLEM. I'm not part of this.

RONNIE. I'll make it worth your while.

SHIRLEY. Hang out, Clem.

(**CLEM** *grumpily sits.*)

RONNIE. *(to* **FEE***)* What about the three lost? Eric, Sandra, Mick. Anything different on them?

FEE. Only that Eric was having a rough shift.

RONNIE. Rough how?

FEE. Panting, tired, used up his water ration early.

RONNIE. Okay now wait a minute. That squares, right?

SHIRLEY. With what?

RONNIE. Well we didn't have eyewitnesses on the first couple explosions, but the third one, on the Gathering Path? Cristobal House Seven was panting, tired, went right though his water.

SHIRLEY. What does that prove?

PECK. That could be any work shift ever.

RONNIE. I don't think so, most people learn to drink slow.

PECK. Plus you don't explode from being thirsty.

RONNIE. Fuck! What am I not thinking of?

SHIRLEY. Well you know, Ronnie, it's supposed to be kind of a group effort.

CLEM. Shit, don't tell her that.

RONNIE. *(to* **PECK***)* What you said about Eric, you said it was like he exploded from the inside?

PECK. Just pieces of him everywhere. Only knew it was him from his head.

SHIRLEY. Could be they're gaslighting us, the bugs, like a trick to draw us out?

RONNIE. It's not the bugs, I know it isn't. It was right there on Abbie's face, he doesn't know, they don't know, they're scared and they *don't know.*

CLEM. But that's just something you think.

RONNIE. What?

CLEM. That's just something you think. That's not something we know. You said we're just supposed to say things we know.

TASH. Hey! Show some respect!

CLEM. For what? What for? What's Ronnie ever done that I should be all respecting about?

TASH. She's a lot braver than you!

CLEM. What's Ronnie ever done except be the daughter of the man who brought them here in the first place?

(ugly beat)

Am I done "hanging out" now?

RONNIE. Say what we know.

CLEM. What?

RONNIE. You just heard the new info, now tell us what we know.

CLEM. I'm not in this!

RONNIE. I told you I'd make it worth your while. You're the smartest in this house. You just watched me hear the whole scoop and come up with nothing. Are you really telling me you're gonna pass up a chance to make me look like an asshole? *(beat)*

CLEM. Four explosions. Two on Coral Farm, two on Gathering Path. Nobody saw the bugs do anything different, nobody saw the Nampas do anything different. At least two times, one of the dead was seen just before out of breath and out of water. Is that it?

RONNIE. What about Eric?

CLEM. Blown up from the inside.

RONNIE. And? Come on. Anything jumping out?

CLEM. No. Can I go to bed now?

RONNIE. One good idea first.

CLEM. How about I just go anyway, and fuck you?

TASH. Coward!

CLEM. The places, all right? What do the places have in common?

RONNIE. What places?

CLEM. Coral and Gathering, where the explosions happened.

FEE. I mean, every place is the same as every other place. Mangroves and water.

RONNIE. Fuck!

TASH. Sorry, Ronnie, I can't think of anything!

SHIRLEY. Everybody needs to dig deep here. We could cut the workday by a quarter.

RONNIE. Oh fuck that, that's nothing.

PECK. There's the smell.

SHIRLEY. *(to* RONNIE*)* You know what, I bet all the people pulling veggies on the farm right this second don't think it's nothing. You wanna go ask them?

RONNIE. We don't want concessions, we want them gone!

TASH. Ronnie's right!

SHIRLEY. Who's we?

RONNIE. *(to* PECK.*)* Wait, what did you say?

PECK. The smell. We haven't figured that in yet.

RONNIE. It's worse, right?

FEE. I think it's worse every year.

PECK. It's that stuff that comes out of them.

TASH. Oh yeah! When they're sucking the juice out of those fleshy flowers?

PECK. Every harvest. When the bugs're drinking out of the fleshies –

FEE. Yeah yeah, and something leaks out of them!

PECK. They have to drain off something inside to make room for the flower juice. Whatever it is gets in the water under the fleshies and smells. Worse this year than I ever remember.

RONNIE. What would be different this yeat?

CLEM. *(half to herself)* 'Cause they're laying eggs...?

RONNIE. What?

CLEM. Nothing.

SHIRLEY. So we think what, it mixes in the water, somehow causes a reaction –

PECK. No, if that's what it was half the Settlement would blow up every harvest.

>   (**CLEM** *exhales impatiently.*)

TASH. Hey! If you don't wanna be here you can fuck right off!

CLEM. I was just gonna say –

TASH. If you don't wanna be in the Resistance at least you can –

CLEM. What "resistance"? You've killed a few bugs, you've killed a few Nampas, and *nothing's ever changed.* They're bigger and stronger and smarter and they all share a brain, and they've *got us*! Shouldn't the smart people quit crying about it and figure out the best way live with it? I'm gonna have a baby!

TASH. I was gonna have a baby.

RONNIE. You were gonna say what?

CLEM. What?

RONNIE. You said, "I was just gonna say." What were you gonna say?

CLEM. I don't know!

RONNIE. Yeah you do.

CLEM. Just…if Eric was thirsty, if he went through his water, if the others went through their water, maybe they snuck under the fleshies to take a drink. Maybe they drank the bad water. Maybe it happens when a person drinks the bad water.

>   (**RONNIE, SHIRLEY**, *and* **PECK** *look at each other for a beat.*)

RONNIE. Motherfucker.

SHIRLEY. Okay, let's just take a minute.

PECK. 'Cause the thing is, to be sure?

SHIRLEY. Enough. Stop right there.

RONNIE. Do you get what this means?

SHIRLEY. Do you?

RONNIE. What if she's right?

CLEM. Can I be done now, please?

RONNIE. We can't drop this, we can't even *stall* it. If she's right we're on the *clock*.

SHIRLEY. I need to think.

RONNIE. One way or another, this will keep happening!

SHIRLEY. I said I need to *think*! Who's in charge here?!

> *(Something hits the roof of the house. Insect legs skitter down the side.)*

FEE. Flyer!

SHIRLEY. *(to PECK)* Clear out. Now.

RONNIE. *(to PECK)* See you later?

PECK. Tell me first.

RONNIE. What?

PECK. You know you're carrying? Find me somewhere and tell me. They're our babies. We made them together. Don't let me hear like that. Tell me first.

RONNIE. Forgive me.

> **(PECK** *kisses her and hurries out through the kitchen.)*

ABBIE. *(through the front door)* House Four?

> **(FEE** *opens the door to reveal* **ABBIE** *and* **CONOR.***)*

SHIRLEY. Come on in, Ambassadors. Nice to see you.

CONOR. *(entering)* Thank you, Shirley House Four –*(He stops when he sees* **RONNIE.***)* Ronnie.

ABBIE. What the fuck are you doing here?

CONOR. I'm pleased to see you!

> **(WILLA** *sits up some more.)*

Excuse me, she's awake.

> *(He hurries past* **RONNIE** *to check on* **WILLA.***)*

RONNIE. *(to ABBIE)* I missed bleeding. By several days. Don't you wanna say something nice?

CONOR. Has she been awake before?

FEE. A little, but she's never tried to sit up like that.

ABBIE. *(to all)* I have an announcement. The Honeycomb has granted me permission to institute a curfew in House Four. All inhabitants of House Four are to be in their beds by sundown. Anyone congregating in this room after sundown is outside the Law.

TASH. You can *fuck* your curfew –

> *(**RONNIE** puts a hand on **TASH**, silencing her.)*

ABBIE. *(to **SHIRLEY**)* Unless – is anyone sleeping down here now?

SHIRLEY. *(indicating **WILLA**)* Just her.

ABBIE. All right, but she does not leave her bed after sundown. Understood? Things are gonna be different here now.

RONNIE. *(to **FEE** and **CLEM**)* Well, girls, I think it's bedtime.

CONOR. *(to **WILLA**)* Sshhh. You don't have to be afraid.

Four

(CONOR teaches WILLA walking. He holds out his arms and she walks unsteadily to him. ABBIE appears at the top of the stairs and watches.)

ABBIE. I remember Mom doing that with you.

CONOR. Just your mother?

ABBIE. Who else?

CONOR. You and Ronnie. You used to do it together. *(meaning AMELIA)* Has she slept?

ABBIE. Little stretches. Never for long.

CONOR. I'll go to her.

ABBIE. No, that's not a good idea, keep working with her. We need her ready.

CONOR. Where are you going?

ABBIE. The Honeycomb. I can't sleep here. She did it deliberately, you know.

CONOR. Ronnie?

ABBIE. To get back in here to plan whatever she's planning in the one place the People won't go. Can you explain that to me? Close on twelve years and they still haven't conquered their revulsion?

CONOR. Imagine seeing live birth for the first time in the history of your civilization.

ABBIE. But twelve years! And they still can't walk through the door we built especially for them?

CONOR. It hasn't been revulsion for a long time.

ABBIE. What, fear?

CONOR. Reverence. The place of the queen is sacred.

ABBIE. Look, I'm not saying kill Ronnie. I should be, if she's doing what I think she is, she shouldn't be special, but all right, I fall short. But we know who she's talking to. Why don't we just kill them?

CONOR. The Honeycomb wants proof.

ABBIE. *(indicating* **WILLA***)* So either Willa gets into the inner circle, or we just have to wait for something to happen?

CONOR. Better that than kill innocent humans. The deal we made with your father was: save our people, and we'll save yours.

ABBIE. Then get her where she needs to be. The sooner they trust her, the sooner we can find out and stop it, and nobody has to think about contingencies. God, the whole point of this –

CONOR. Contingencies?

ABBIE. The whole point was peace, so I could get some peace, but there hasn't been peace for a minute.

CONOR. What contingencies?

ABBIE. I'll stay out of your way. You know what you're doing. I don't.

CONOR. Abbie, wait.

> *(He makes sure* **WILLA***'s stable, then goes to* **ABBIE** *at the door.)*

Are you all right?

> *(Behind them, over the following,* **WILLA** *takes a tentative step away from the wall. She totters, but maintains her balance.)*

ABBIE. What do the People of the Honeycomb ask themselves at the end of their lives?

CONOR. What small thing did I do to help build the Honeycomb?

ABBIE. So, I'm doing it. So I'm fine.

> *(He kisses* **CONOR** *and leaves.* **CONOR** *notices* **WILLA***.)*

CONOR. Are you…all right? Are you going to fall?

> *(She holds out her arms to him: she wants to walk again.)*

CONOR. You're remarkable.

(She walks to him, gestures that she wants to go again.)

CONOR. Yes, yes, of course.

*(**CONOR** crosses the room; she walks to him again. **AMELIA** comes partway down the stairs. As **WILLA** reaches **CONOR** he backs away.)*

CONOR. Keep coming. Do more than you think you can. You can do more than you think.

*(He notices **AMELIA**.)*

CONOR. Amelia.

*(She makes her way down the stairs, watching **WILLA**.)*

CONOR. Abbie thought… He left because he thought you were asleep.

AMELIA. *(to **WILLA**)* Look at me.

*(**WILLA** turns to the sound of **AMELIA**'s voice. **AMELIA** studies her.)*

CONOR. I'm helping her remember how to walk.

AMELIA. Dying doesn't make you stupid.

*(**CONOR** realizes she knows.)*

She's had enough. She needs to sit down.

CONOR. *(leading **WILLA** to her cot)* I'm sure you're right.

*(He sets **WILLA** down.)*

AMELIA. Everybody thinks you're the only one.

CONOR. I hate lying. It's like a pain that never subsides.

AMELIA. I know all about it.

CONOR. If you tell them, they'll kill her. We won't be able to prove it. We'll just find her somewhere. Or not find her at all.

AMELIA. I imagine that's true.

CONOR. I swear to you, she's not in this house to hurt your daughter.

AMELIA. Then why?

CONOR. They're setting off bombs, killing people, yours and mine. We don't know how. If Willa can find out, we can stop them.

AMELIA. And Ronnie?

CONOR. We don't want to punish Ronnie. We just want to stop her from hurting us.

AMELIA. What is your promise worth, Ambassador?

CONOR. Everything.

>(**AMELIA** *has an attack of pain.*)

Oh – oh, Amelia, do you –

AMELIA. *(recovering)* At least Bill was smart enough to die fast.

CONOR. That was a terrible day.

AMELIA. I should ask for something. Shouldn't I? In exchange for my silence.

CONOR. I would do it anyway.

AMELIA. I want a lot of things. But there's really only enough time left for one.

CONOR. You're not dying.

AMELIA. So I want my daughter and son to love each other again. I've decided I don't care about anything else.

CONOR. If we can find the bombs, the resistance ends. They don't have to fight anymore. All you have to do is nothing.

AMELIA. Then… I suppose…it's a deal.

CONOR. Amelia, I never thought to betray you.

AMELIA. Don't. Please.

CONOR. I would have died without your kindness.

>(**AMELIA** *seizes up with pain and staggers.* **CONOR** *hurries to her, holds her up, holds her steady while she recovers.*)

AMELIA. I need to go back to my bed.

CONOR. Of course.

AMELIA. Looks too far to walk from here.

CONOR. I'll teach you.

Five

(Day. **SHIRLEY**, **RONNIE**, *and* **PECK** *watch* **TASH** *study a glass bottle.)*

TASH. It's glass, right?

SHIRLEY. It is.

TASH. Haven't seen it green since Before. From the Memory stash, right?

SHIRLEY. That's right.

TASH. I was on Memory duty once. They had me hiding the two little bottles, medicine or something. I kept 'em both in my snatch and the bugs never guessed.

(She gives the bottle back to **SHIRLEY**.*)*

It's beautiful.

SHIRLEY. Tash, why did you come here today?

TASH. Word is, House Four needs a job.

SHIRLEY. That's right.

TASH. I'm ready.

SHIRLEY. I haven't told you what it is.

TASH. I'm ready for anything.

SHIRLEY. Tash, we need you to…we want to ask you to…

TASH. What?

SHIRLEY. You know I wouldn't ask you to do anything that I…

(She looks at **RONNIE**.*)*

RONNIE. Hey Tash, why don't we take a little break?

TASH. I don't wanna take a break, I'm ready.

RONNIE. *(sitting next to her)* How're you holding up, Tash?

TASH. I'm good, I'm ready.

RONNIE. Really?

TASH. I mean…it's hard. I had a man, I was gonna have a baby.

SHIRLEY. Oh, Tash…

RONNIE. I'm sorry about your man, too.

TASH. I'm not. Nampas piece of shit.

RONNIE. But your baby was good. Your baby was pure goodness. World hadn't put a hand on her.

TASH. You know, I watch you, Ronnie.

RONNIE. What do you wanna do that for?

TASH. You keep moving. Nothing hurts you.

RONNIE. You know I was saying to Shirley, I just keep thinking, it would've been so different before the bugs, *(to* SHIRLEY*)* isn't that right?

SHIRLEY. Tash, you have to understand, we used to have machines, we could watch the baby, we could listen to its heart...we'd have something more than choopie for the pain.

RONNIE. And if you couldn't turn the baby...

SHIRLEY. We could cut you. Get out the baby, keep you from being infected, keep you both alive.

RONNIE. But all those machines, all that medicine Shirley's talking about? That could keep every other woman from ever feeling like you feel right now? It's all out there. Right now. Right under the mud. Waiting for us, the second the bugs are gone.

TASH. What do you need me to do?

> (RONNIE *rises and holds out her hand to* SHIRLEY *for the bottle. A beat.* SHIRLEY *hands the bottle to* RONNIE.)

RONNIE. Peck here's gonna take you to Gathering Path, where the water pools under the fleshies.

TASH. The smelly water.

RONNIE. *(holding up the bottle)* And you're gonna take this with you.

> (TASH *figures it out.*)

You understand?

TASH. Yeah.

RONNIE. Tash...

TASH. I'm ready.

RONNIE. Your life is important.

TASH. I know. I wanna use it for this. *(beat)*

PECK. After we get the water we'll find a quiet spot out east. When I say, you're gonna count to a hundred, and then you're gonna drink.

TASH. Let's do it.

PECK. Not right now, in a day or two. When I tell you.

SHIRLEY. Then what?

PECK. If it goes the way we think, I'll have to move fast: get in there, pace out the blast radius, and get out before the bugs get there.

SHIRLEY. The blast radius?

PECK. The distance affected by the explosion. How far from the source it tears things up.

TASH. You've got such a good man, Ronnie. You can tell just to look at him, he's such good big man.

RONNIE. C'mere, Tash. *(RONNIE pulls TASH into an embrace.)* When the day comes that the bugs are gone and we're remembering how we did it, we're gonna say it all started with Tash House Five, and a bottle of green glass.

TASH. I love you so much.

PECK. All right, we gotta move.

TASH. Where are we going?

PECK. Somewhere we can practice counting. Need to make sure that you and me count to one hundred at exactly the same time.

TASH. Let's go right now!

PECK. Sounds good.

> *(He kisses RONNIE.)*

TASH. I'll be perfect. Oh Ronnie!

> *(TASH hugs RONNIE again, then follows PECK out.)*

SHIRLEY. If it works…if it goes like we think…

RONNIE. Ah, fuck.

SHIRLEY. 'Cause right now it's just a theory. But if it *works…*
    (beat) Maybe it won't work.

RONNIE. It has to.

Six

(Evening. **AMELIA** *is on the couch, draped in blankets.* **FEE** *tries to give her some water.* **WILLA** *sits up in her cot.* **SHIRLEY** *watches* **RONNIE** *pace and check the windows.)*

AMELIA. Not thirsty.

FEE. You sure look thirsty.

SHIRLEY. *(to* **RONNIE***)* That's probably not helping.

RONNIE. You think they got there yet?

SHIRLEY. Probably would've heard something.

RONNIE. I don't mean did they *do* it, I mean did they *get there* yet?

SHIRLEY. So you want me to guess.

AMELIA. Ronnie.

RONNIE. He's coming, Mom.

AMELIA. He told you himself?

RONNIE. No he didn't fucking tell me himself, remember how phones don't exist anymore? He sent someone ahead on a flyer.

AMELIA. I want to see him the minute he comes in.

RONNIE. Do you ask for me like this when I'm not here?

AMELIA. You're always here.

> *(***RONNIE*** throws up her hands and goes to* **SHIRLEY***.)*

RONNIE. This is a mistake.

SHIRLEY. It is what it is.

RONNIE. We can't be tiptoeing around Abbie and Skin all night, we need to be able to work!

SHIRLEY. My mom's probably dead. I'll never get to Cincinnati, I'll never find out, but she had heart trouble *before* the bugs.

RONNIE. You'll get to Cincinnati. I swear you will.

SHIRLEY. Go sit with your mom.

RONNIE. If Peck doesn't come back…

SHIRLEY. Come on, it's Peck.

RONNIE. Only reason I get out of bed in the morning.

SHIRLEY. That's bullshit.

RONNIE. I can't feel both things at once.

SHIRLEY. Except I'm watching you do it.

RONNIE. He doesn't know they're here! What if he tries to come back here tonight?

SHIRLEY. I've got a runner coming by. We'll send her east, she'll intercept him.

RONNIE. I need to talk to her first. I need to give her a message for him.

SHIRLEY. Fine.

RONNIE. Thank you, Shirley.

> (**SHIRLEY** *acknowledges.*)

I'm sorry about the way I am.

SHIRLEY. Sit with your Mom.

> (**RONNIE** *goes to the couch.*)

RONNIE. Okay, Fee.

> (*She takes the water from* **FEE**, *who exits to the kitchen.*)

Thirsty, Mom?

AMELIA. You too?

RONNIE. Gotta tell you, Mom, you look rough. I'm not kidding.

> (*They're both amused, but then* **AMELIA** *gets quiet.*)

AMELIA. I'm not leaving anything behind. Even your father left something behind.

RONNIE. Shitty example, Mom.

AMELIA. But not me.

RONNIE. Well, two kids, but I guess…

AMELIA. It'll be like I never lived. (*beat*) Say it.

RONNIE. Say what?

AMELIA. If I'd gone to the police, if I'd stopped him, then my life would have meaning.

RONNIE. What is this meaning shit?

AMELIA. But I already thought that through. He'd have found a way. And all the armies in the world couldn't stop them. That's what it is: not regret, not shame: but that it couldn't have been any different. So what am I supposed to tell you now?

SHIRLEY. Flyer!

> (*We hear the insect landing, the skittering of its legs.*)

AMELIA. (*rising up on her elbows*) Abbie?

SHIRLEY. Probably.

RONNIE. What, you're sitting up now?

AMELIA. Is that Abbie?

RONNIE. (*to* **SHIRLEY**) Where's that fucking runner?

SHIRLEY. She's coming.

RONNIE. How am I supposed to do this?

SHIRLEY. Like you do everything. Pretend you can until you can.

> (**RONNIE** *opens the door.* **ABBIE** *and* **CONOR** *enter.*)

ABBIE. Where is she?

> (**RONNIE** *steps back and indicates* **AMELIA**.)

Why isn't she in her room?

RONNIE. Cooler down here.

AMELIA. Abbie?

ABBIE. Hey, Mom. Hey Mom, how are you?

AMELIA. Abbie, come over to me.

ABBIE. (*going to her*) Mom, is your room –

> (*She hugs him.*)

AMELIA. Abbie.

ABBIE. Mom if your room's too hot we can –

AMELIA. I was hot. Now I'm cold.

ABBIE. Well let's take you back up. I'll call some Nampas.

RONNIE. You're going to bring a pack of Nampas in this house to carry our mother around.

ABBIE. She said she was cold!

FEE. I'll pull a blanket off somebody. *(She exits up the stairs.)*

AMELIA. I suppose I should make you take hands. Make peace with each other. A deathbed oath.

ABBIE. It's not your deathbed Mom, come on.

AMELIA. But I'm not a fool.

RONNIE. Why can't it be her deathbed?

ABBIE. What?

RONNIE. "Death is not death. To be digested by the Honeycomb, to be restored to the soil, is to transmute death into new life."

ABBIE. That's right, sneer. And then explain why it's wrong.

RONNIE. Then she can die. And we can take her bundle of bones to the Honeycomb for digestion.

ABBIE. They don't *eat* them, they put them back in the soil – you *know* that!

AMELIA. *Please.*

     (beat)

ABBIE. I'm sorry, Mom.

CONOR. Amelia, can we make you more comfortable in any way?

RONNIE. Now you care about comfortable?

ABBIE. But you see how angry she makes me, I mean you see, right?

AMELIA. *(to RONNIE)* He needed me more than you. Can you understand that?

ABBIE. That's not true.

RONNIE. Fuck this. *(She goes to a window.)*

AMELIA. Until he didn't.

ABBIE. That's not true, don't talk about me like that.

AMELIA. *(peering at* **CONOR***)* Not as much as he did. Him more than anyone.

ABBIE. *(to* **RONNIE***)* Looking for something?

RONNIE. You know what, maybe you should be paying attention to Mom instead of me.

ABBIE. I should pay attention to Mom?

CONOR. Abbie, not now.

RONNIE. Instead of obsessing over every little thing I do.

ABBIE. *(overlapping)* I should pay attention to Mom? I did everything for Mom! She got to keep her own room in her own house! She didn't have to work on the farms! I made them dam it up with floodwalls so she could live here!

RONNIE. Why?

ABBIE. I put the carrying women in here so she'd have Shirley to look after her! I did all that, that was me!

RONNIE. Why, though? If nobody's special, why did you do it?

SHIRLEY. Ronnie, let it go.

> *(***AMELIA***'s pain gets more intense.* **CONOR** *notices.)*

ABBIE. What do you ever do but leave her all night so you can run around murdering anyone you feel like?

CONOR. Amelia!

> *(He goes to* **AMELIA** *and she grips him, hard.)*

ABBIE. What is it? What's wrong with her?

AMELIA. Oh *god*!

ABBIE. We should – maybe we can – maybe –

RONNIE. What, give her painkillers?

ABBIE. Even now, even *now*, you can't *stop*!?

> *(There is a massive explosion in the distance.)*

What was that?

> *(He runs to the window.)*

Where was it, which way?

CONOR. *(still with* **AMELIA***)* East, I think.

ABBIE. *(to* **RONNIE***)* Tonight, *tonight,* you do this.

RONNIE. Do what?

ABBIE. I've got to get there now. Before they get away.

CONOR. Abbie.

ABBIE. The flyer. The flyer can get me there and back. We can't just let this keep happening! *(to* **AMELIA***)* I'm gonna be right back, okay? *(to* **RONNIE***)* If I connect this with you, I promise, if I connect this with you –

RONNIE. Why don't you go pretend to fly?

> (**ABBIE** *storms out the front door. Sounds of the insect taking off.* **FEE** *enters from the kitchen and signals significantly to* **SHIRLEY**.)

SHIRLEY. *(to* **RONNIE**.*)* The runner's here.

RONNIE. Right now?

> (**FEE** *nods.*)

'Kay Mom, be right back.

> (*She exits after* **SHIRLEY** *and* **FEE**.)

AMELIA. Did I hurt you?

CONOR. Not at all.

AMELIA. Got me all to yourself.

CONOR. They're returning very soon.

AMELIA. When it was my mom's time I didn't want to be there either.

CONOR. They're coming back.

AMELIA. I never should have taken them with me. They were so small, they didn't understand. She was bald. She was so thin. She looked like a monster. Face like a monster. And Abbie drew it, over and over again. "The Bald Woman." I didn't know how to tell him to stop.

CONOR. Try to rest.

AMELIA. You have to look out for him. He's like his father. He falls in love with phantoms.

CONOR. Amelia, may I speak with you? In your position as Abbie's mother?

AMELIA. My position?

CONOR. It's true that I have nothing. I don't own the clothes I wear. I don't even own the body underneath them, not really. I have nothing to offer your Abbie but the wisdom of my people and the love in my heart. But I ask you to consider: my people plucked me out of millions crawling in the hive and said, "You will be Ambassador. You will speak for us." I have forged the strength of my character through the destruction of my home-world and across the vastness of space, and I offer that strength to your son for both our lifetimes.

AMELIA. I was wrong about you.

(**RONNIE, SHIRLEY,** *and* **FEE** *enter.*)

SHIRLEY. Look: She's fast, she knows the canal.

RONNIE. All *right.* *(But she's looking at* **AMELIA.**)

SHIRLEY. You can count on her.

RONNIE. *(looking at* **AMELIA**) What is she...? Her head's funny.

CONOR. Amelia.

RONNIE. Let me see her.

SHIRLEY. Let *me* see her.

CONOR. Amelia!

(**SHIRLEY** *checks* **AMELIA***'s pulse. Beat.*)

Tell me. Tell me!

(**SHIRLEY** *looks at* **RONNIE** *and shakes her head.*)

But...

RONNIE. All right, Conor, we have to –

CONOR. Amelia!

RONNIE. Conor, we –

(*She stops as* **CONOR** *pulls the dead* **AMELIA** *up into an embrace. He rocks her back and forth.*)

Conor, we have to wrap her up.

CONOR. No.

RONNIE. We have to get her ready.

CONOR. You can't.

RONNIE. We have to take her to the Honeycomb. It's Law. It's *your* Law.

CONOR. You can't. You can't have her. You can't.

Seven

(ABBIE enters to find RONNIE looking through an old box of drawings.)

RONNIE. This is all that was in her room. You want it?

ABBIE. I'm sorry you couldn't join us.

RONNIE. I mean, you were grinding Mom into compost, right?

ABBIE. The reconstituting process. I think it's one of the most beautiful things I've ever seen. New life springing out of death; nature doesn't get much more generous than that. So yes, I'm genuinely sorry you didn't see it today.

RONNIE. *(handing him the box)* You want it or not?

ABBIE. *(glancing through the photos)* God, look at these.

RONNIE. Yeah, it seems like million years…

ABBIE. I was going to *draw. That* was going to be my life. Can you imagine?

(He hands RONNIE a drawing.)

Look. Remember? The Bald Woman?

RONNIE. No.

ABBIE. Are you sure? "I saw the Bald Woman! She's on the porch!" Look at it again.

RONNIE. I've looked at it.

ABBIE. Fine, but you totally remember. *(He sets the box down.)*

RONNIE. You seem…

ABBIE. What?

RONNIE. Hey: best mood I've seen on you in years, I'm not gonna mess with it.

ABBIE. I'm not happy she's gone. But I'm a little bit happy about what it means.

RONNIE. What it means?

ABBIE. And I sort of think you are, too. *(beat)*

RONNIE. We're done, right?

ABBIE. Exactly.

RONNIE. We're not anything to each other. We can just sort of be enemies…

ABBIE. And it's fine.

RONNIE. Almost like we should shake on it.

ABBIE. We can if you want.

>   *(beat)*

RONNIE. Heading back to the Honeycomb?

ABBIE. When I'm done here.

RONNIE. I don't get it, how do you – do they have like a bunk set up for you there?

ABBIE. Of course not. I sleep anywhere I lie down.

RONNIE. And nobody steps on you?

ABBIE. Never. It's like a miracle. You ever notice how human bodies – we can hold each other, and it feels beautiful for a while, but then our bodies overheat, and we have to separate? The People of the Honeycomb crawl in, around, among, between, atop, below one another all day and night. It should be a tangled mess, but it's not, it works. When I get close to the center, I can lie down, close my eyes, and just hear the sounds, feel the antennae, feel the legs, and no one ever steps on me. They're so delicate.

RONNIE. And at the center?

ABBIE. Are you gathering intelligence, Ronnie?

RONNIE. You can answer or not.

ABBIE. I can't get to the center. Not enough air.

RONNIE. So you've never seen the queen.

ABBIE. I've heard her. I can get close enough to hear her. But you know what the best part is?

RONNIE. Look, I haven't slept in –

ABBIE. That it's not here. That I'm not still sleeping *here*, where I grew up, where I drew those *(indicating the box)*, where I thought that's what I was gonna be. That's what you need.

RONNIE. Me?

ABBIE. You need to get out of here, Ronnie. You wanna spend your life here? Looking for Dad in the corners so you can fight a rematch?

RONNIE. Okay, what the fuck is happening right now?

ABBIE. I flew to the bomb site last night, looked at that poor woman's shredded body, and what did I feel? Not outrage for the murder. Fear for *you*. Know why I didn't come straight back after? 'Cause I was at the Honeycomb pleading for *you*.

RONNIE. Pleading for what?

ABBIE. We're sending you away. You can stay 'til the baby. After the baby, a flyer will take you to Savannah Farm. There'll be a house and a cot and a detail waiting for you there.

RONNIE. Savannah?

ABBIE. Of course I would urge you to use the remaining time here to –

RONNIE. I want my husband with me. I want –

ABBIE. You don't have a husband.

RONNIE. I want my kids.

ABBIE. You never see your kids, and you don't have a husband.

RONNIE. I want them transferred with me.

ABBIE. What church were you married in?

RONNIE. Well there you go.

ABBIE. Sure, you should get married. You should keep your kids in a house with you, you should live together, and prefer each other to anyone else. Eventually you should decide that you love each other so much that if it came to a choice, you'd be willing to hurt other people for the crime of not living in your house. How is that a sane way to live?

RONNIE. You can keep trying, you're never gonna sound like Dad.

ABBIE. This is me saving your life! You know what we're gonna do if this doesn't stop?

RONNIE. What?

ABBIE. You should be thanking me!

RONNIE. Wait. What are you talking about?

ABBIE. No one's going with you. You're going alone. *(beat)*

RONNIE. You can't.

ABBIE. We can.

RONNIE. Look, Abbie, send me away if you have to, but come on, you can send Peck, what does it hurt?

ABBIE. Sure, maybe I should send your whole pack of killers with you, you could pick right up in Savannah.

RONNIE. He's all I've got.

ABBIE. We're giving you what, six, seven months? Why don't you use them to –

RONNIE. He's my life.

ABBIE. Then look at me, and tell me, truthfully, that you'll stop. *(beat)* You have until the baby.

RONNIE. Forgot your box.

ABBIE. Don't want it.

RONNIE. She saved this for you. All your drawings, everything, this whole time.

ABBIE. Throw them out. I don't want them.

(*He exits.* **RONNIE** *watches him go for a beat, then –*)

RONNIE. I can hear you.

(**PECK** *enters from the kitchen.*)

You're lucky he didn't.

PECK. Wasn't your brother I'd break him in half.

RONNIE. Pick me up.

PECK. Yeah?

RONNIE. I need to be nothing for a minute. I need to be in the air.

(**PECK** *goes to her. He scoops her up in his arms and lifts her off the ground.*)

She's gone.

PECK. I got you.

> *(**SHIRLEY** comes partway down the stairs. To **SHIRLEY**.)*

It's okay.

RONNIE. Tell me.

PECK. Sure?

RONNIE. Just tell me.

PECK. Ten paces. *(beat)*

RONNIE. Put me down.

> *(**PECK** sets her down.)*

SHIRLEY. Ten paces radius? That's a lot.

PECK. Walked it myself.

RONNIE. Have we paced out the base of the Honeycomb?

SHIRLEY. Ronnie.

RONNIE. Have we?

PECK. Five hundred eight.

RONNIE. *(pointing at part of the wall)* Run the numbers.

> *(**PECK** goes to a secret stash in the wall, gets some paper and a crayon.)*

SHIRLEY. What the hell are you doing? Who told you that was there?

> *(**PECK** starts drawing.)*

PECK. 'Kay, ten pace radius, twenty pace diameter…

SHIRLEY. Now you're writing this down?

PECK. To be safe… I'd say twenty-six on the outside, and… I mean, twenty-two for those interior supports. If we wanna be safe.

RONNIE. *(taking the crayon)* Plus three at the center. For the Queen.

SHIRLEY. You know what they'll do if they find that?

PECK. We don't know she's at the center.

RONNIE. We do now.

PECK. So fifty-one.

(He rips the paper into small shreds. **RONNIE** *returns the rest to the stash.)*

SHIRLEY. Okay – wait – fifty-one…people?

PECK. Just walk into the bottom level like we're on shift…

RONNIE. Exactly, like it's a normal day, and then…

SHIRLEY. Hey! Both of you! Don't you get what's on offer here?

RONNIE. Fuck their offer.

SHIRLEY. Fuck a quarter off the working day? Fuck three less hours on the farm? Can I tell people you said so?

RONNIE. Quarter off if the explosions stop.

SHIRLEY. Exactly!

RONNIE. Which means we have to tell everybody. People we trust, people we don't, Nampas, anyone who could drink. Then it gets back to the bugs, they secure the water, and the only weapon *we'll ever have* is gone forever. Are you ready to make that call? For *everyone?*

SHIRLEY. This isn't a weapon, this is…

PECK. Sure it is. What else does a weapon do?

(Over the following, **WILLA** *sits up in bed.)*

SHIRLEY. Ronnie, I've been running this resistance close to ten years now. I'm older than anyone you know. You think I don't know what I'm doing?

RONNIE. You put the word out, it's as good as saying this is how it's always gonna be.

SHIRLEY. This *is* how it's always gonna be! *(pause)*

RONNIE. Or I find fifty-one.

SHIRLEY. From where?

RONNIE. From people we trust.

SHIRLEY. That's what? Three hundred heads? Less?

RONNIE. I'll get them. Because I have to. I've got 'til the baby.

SHIRLEY. You won't even get one! No one's gonna do that!

RONNIE. Give me 'til the baby. I don't get fifty-one by the baby, we forget it, they ship me off, it's over. But I *do* get them? I *do* get fifty-one? That's when I bring it all down. Shirley: you *know* you don't have a better bet than me.

WILLA. Aaaaaaaah!

RONNIE. Fuck!

(They all turn to WILLA.)

WILLA. Aaaaaaaaaah!

SHIRLEY. Holy shit, are you talking?

WILLA. Nnnnn…

SHIRLEY. You're trying to talk, aren't you?

(SHIRLEY goes to WILLA, touches her supportively.)

WILLA. Nnnnnnnnnnaaah!

SHIRLEY. Well I'll be damned. Welcome back. *(to RONNIE)* Do it.

(Lights down.)

End of Act One

ACT TWO

Eight

(Early evening. Six months have passed since the end of Act One. JIMMY *sits next to* FEE, *facing* RONNIE *and* SHIRLEY. RONNIE *is heavily pregnant.* PECK *is between* JIMMY *and the door.)*

RONNIE. Say anything you wanna say, Jimmy.

JIMMY. You mean, like… "No"? What's up with "No"? You like "No"? *(to* FEE*)* Right? Right? "No." Do it with me: "No." *(beat)* Fee. Girl. *(beat)*

FEE. *(to* JIMMY.*)* Baby.

JIMMY. Aw, no, no, no, come on, man, come on. This is stupid. This is so stupid.

FEE. I know it's scary, baby.

JIMMY. What's scary? There's no "scary," it's just, "No." Real simple. Here's you: "Drink some poison and blow up!" Here's me: "No." Done.

FEE. You don't hate them?

JIMMY. Who?

FEE. The bugs!

JIMMY. I hate *lots* of things! This is crazy! No, you know what, this is *stupid.*

FEE. They didn't leave us anything else to fight them with. This is all we've got.

JIMMY. Are you doing it?

SHIRLEY. Fee's carrying.

JIMMY. Oh, "Fee's carrying," so that's like, that's like…

SHIRLEY. We need every baby. You know how it is, two of yours didn't make it out of cradle.

FEE. One with me, one with that other girl.

JIMMY. *(sharply, to* FEE*)* What?

SHIRLEY. We need every baby.

JIMMY. Yeah! I get it! Every baby! What, are you doing it? With your dried up ass? You got any more babies coming?

SHIRLEY. Yeah. I'm doing it. *(pause)*

JIMMY. Man, this is just – this is just *stupid.*

(**WILLA** *appears on the stairs.*)

WILLA. Hello.

RONNIE. Willa?

WILLA. I woke up.

RONNIE. Well lie down, you'll probably go right back to sleep.

WILLA. I really don't think I can make myself sleep anymore.

SHIRLEY. *(to* **RONNIE***)* I got it.

WILLA. You think I could hang out down here with you guys?

SHIRLEY. Why don't I come up and talk to you?

WILLA. Well…do you guys need any help?

SHIRLEY. With what?

WILLA. I just want to do something.

SHIRLEY. Talking's doing something. Come and talk to me upstairs. I can't get over you talking.

(*She leads* **WILLA** *up the stairs.* **JIMMY** *gets up to leave.*)

JIMMY. All right, that's it.

(*He stands.* **PECK** *does too.*)

Oh, what, you're not gonna let me go?

PECK. You can go.

JIMMY. I feel like you're gonna…

PECK. What?

(**JIMMY** *stares at* **PECK.** **RONNIE** *nods to* **FEE.***)*

FEE. Jimmy.

JIMMY. *What?* I feel like I'm crazy, like it's coming from everywhere: I got *him*, I got *her*, I got *you*, it's like...

FEE. I just wanna say I forgive you. *(pause)*

JIMMY. Like...what? Wait, what?

FEE. I was mad for a while, I was hurt, but that's over, and I forgive you.

JIMMY. You forgive me.

FEE. I do.

JIMMY. Man...everybody fucks a bunch of people! Everybody's got babies with everybody!

FEE. Not everybody, but you're right, lots of people.

JIMMY. I couldn't get in here, you know, bugs keeping watch, Nampas keeping watch, and I just got like... Girl, you know I'd go to you first.

FEE. Yeah, *first.*

JIMMY. See right there? See right there? But you "forgive" me, right?

FEE. I don't mean anything by it.

JIMMY. I don't even talk to that girl anymore!

FEE. You should, you got a baby with her!

JIMMY. See right there? This is what it is! Right there!

RONNIE. What do you mean?

JIMMY. *(to* **RONNIE***)* What're you, like, watching?

RONNIE. When you say "This is what it is," what do you mean?

JIMMY. *(indicating* **FEE***)* Right there, look! Ever since she found out about that girl: that face. Like I'm nothing. Like I'm not a man, like I'm nothing. Go ahead and blow myself up, blow up nothing. I don't even talk to that girl anymore!

RONNIE. Jimmy, the Fifty-One are going to be the greatest heroes in the history of the world.

JIMMY. Man don't start that shit.

RONNIE. The greatest heroes in the world. When the bugs are gone and we can build our own things again, the first thing we're gonna build is a great big monument to The Fifty-One. But you don't care about that, right?

JIMMY. Man, "monument"?

RONNIE. You don't care about that. What I hear is, you smoke choopie all night, you get lashed damn near every day 'cause you can't hardly work, and you chase snatch like it's dinner. It's like you're trying to fill every single minute so it's never quiet enough to think. What are you trying not to think about? *(pause)*

JIMMY. *(to FEE.)* The way I thought about it was, I'd hit a couple other girls and then come back to you. In my head it was like I'd always come back to you.

FEE. I don't think you're nothing. You *make* yourself nothing. You could stop that. *(pause)*

JIMMY. When would it be?

RONNIE. We're at forty. We go as soon as we hit fifty-one.

JIMMY. *(to FEE)* That would be the real shit, right? You wouldn't think that was in me.

FEE. I'd be amazed.

JIMMY. That's right, you'd be *amazed.* Would you fuck me every night until it's time to go?

FEE. Every night we can sneak you in.

JIMMY. And then after you fuck me, you'd look at me like you did before that girl?

FEE. Yeah, Jimmy.

JIMMY. That would be the real shit, right? Jimmy House Fourteen says, "Hey bugs, guess what?" *(He makes an exploding sound.)* That was Jimmy House Fourteen!

RONNIE. Jimmy, I would be honored to add your name to The Fifty-One.

JIMMY. Let's do this. *(He makes another exploding sound.)*

RONNIE. Well then I'm very pleased to meet a hero.

PECK. Proud of you, kid.

JIMMY. Shit, you never said that before! *(to FEE.)* Right? Right?

FEE. I'm so proud of you, baby.

JIMMY. Man, I feel like – I just feel like – girl we should fuck right *now*.

FEE. What?

JIMMY. You said! You just said!

FEE. Right here?

JIMMY. *(to* RONNIE *and* PECK*)* You can keep watch, right?

FEE. Boy, go upstairs to my room. You're so stupid.

JIMMY. You go upstairs!

FEE. You go first, I'm coming.

JIMMY. Yeah? You ready for *this?*

FEE. Get up there. So stupid.

JIMMY. *(bounding up the stairs)* Yeah, you're gonna see how stupid I am in a *minute. (He exits. A beat.)*

RONNIE. You okay?

FEE. I've watched you do it lots of times. I just haven't been part of it before.

RONNIE. You did really well.

FEE. I just did what you said.

RONNIE. I just look really hard at people and see what's there. Anybody can do it.

FEE. Then how come nobody else does?

RONNIE. *(indicating up the stairs)* You up for this?

FEE. I do still like him. More like a kid than a man now, but it'll be okay.

(FEE *exits up the stairs.)*

RONNIE. We've gotta move faster.

PECK. Forty-one might bring it down.

RONNIE. We can't swing and miss.

PECK. We've got time yet. The Honeycomb'll keep.

RONNIE. We don't have time. We can't give the ones we've got time to change their minds.

PECK. We can't talk to just anybody. Some folks'll go straight to the Nampas.

RONNIE. What about Cubano Settlement? That's a whole population we haven't touched.

PECK. Miles of open marshland. We'd never get them here.

RONNIE. Fuck! *(pause)*

PECK. It weakens us that I'm not one.

RONNIE. Shirley's one.

PECK. People know it's not the same.

RONNIE. I think you can shut the fuck up.

PECK. Well, I'd like to live, sure, it's nice. But not to see our babies lashed on the farm for taking an extra rest.

RONNIE. I can find ten.

PECK. All right.

RONNIE. I'll find ten.

PECK. All right.

RONNIE. And you never say that shit again.

Nine

(Day. **ABBIE** *and* **WILLA** *practice fighting with reapers.* **CONOR** *enters.)*

CONOR. Stop that! *(They stop and look at him.)* You musn't do that.

ABBIE. We "musn't"?

CONOR. At her stage of pregnancy, Abbie, please, it's too much exertion.

ABBIE. *(to* **WILLA,** *taking the reaper from her)* Was he always such a drag?

WILLA. Always. *(to* **CONOR***)* Where are they?

CONOR. They're taking a turn in the longboat. We have a little time. Now Willa, as a courtesy, please sit down.

WILLA. You know why they go out in the longboat, don't you?

ABBIE. To make plans where no one can hear them.

WILLA. Yes! Oh, I can't stand this! To be stunted like this, so far from readiness!

CONOR. You need to rest.

WILLA. I'm losing my mind with rest! There's nothing I hate in this whole savage language more then "rest"!

CONOR. I'm only speaking of the baby.

ABBIE. *(to* **CONOR***)* All right, you're right. *(He puts the reapers away over the following.)*

WILLA. They sometimes lose the babies, yes? Before the live birth?

CONOR. Miscarriage.

WILLA. The women here don't use that word.

CONOR. It's fallen out of use. It's from Before.

WILLA. Yet it still survives in your books. *(pause)* A decision was made to indulge you.

ABBIE. I spoke for you.

CONOR. When?

WILLA. A decision was made that the information you gleaned from your hidden books might one day compensate for the implication.

CONOR. What implication?

WILLA. That the first time in our history that one of us had an opportunity to keep a secret, he did.

CONOR. You hide your identity from the women of this house. That's a secret.

WILLA. Not a secret to the Honeycomb. Not a secret that matters.

CONOR. It's a short journey. You'll learn that. The habit of secrets is an expanding one. Success at one secret drives you to another, then another, and before you know it your head is full of storms.

WILLA. My head is full of storms?

CONOR. Did I teach you about metaphors?

WILLA. Not why we would use them when there's no one around to hear.

ABBIE. What are we arguing for?

WILLA. Can miscarriage be forced?

CONOR. Forced?

WILLA. Externally triggered? Maybe by injuring the fetus?

CONOR. Willa.

WILLA. I've tolerated everything else. I'll even tolerate this, if need be, but I thought…

CONOR. Maintaining the baby is necessary to maintaining your presence in this house.

ABBIE. He's right.

WILLA. But that's not why you don't want me to do it. You don't want the baby to die.

CONOR. All right. Yes.

WILLA. I don't see how it's possible. I look at the body, I put my fingers in the orifice, and I don't see how it's possible.

ABBIE. You'd find it much easier if you could bring yourselves to watch. No, this is a real problem, this needs focus. You haven't been around the world, I have. At every farm in the world, resistance always makes its home in the house of carrying women.

CONOR. The place of the queen is sacred.

WILLA. The place of the queen is sacred.

ABBIE. Yes, I think I've heard it one or two times before, but the fact of the matter is it makes you sick! It makes me sick too, but you have to be able to witness it or you're making an easy home for sedition!

WILLA. I'll witness *this* one, won't I? In every way possible! I think that will be enough! *(beat)* It won't matter much longer anyway.

ABBIE. No, you're right.

CONOR. What won't matter?

WILLA. The body is everything now. Now that I can't hear the Honeycomb? Now that I'm in this flesh? I never thought of my body before, but now: I must not be too hot. I must not be too cold. I must find a way to sleep at night, though the baby makes it impossible, because I need *so much sleep.* I must not get hurt. I must not die. I, I, *I, I!*

CONOR. We knew what we were agreeing to.

WILLA. No, actually, not true. *I* knew. You didn't. When you spoke to those first humans on Mars, through the man Conor's throat, you had every reason to believe the transition was temporary, and your real body would be waiting for you when negotiations were done. How can you bear it? You never agreed to this…a word, I need a word…

CONOR. Exile?

WILLA. Well of course you would have one. I feel the air on my skin every second. I feel like if it moved with any more force, it would puncture me.

ABBIE. You should show her.

CONOR. Show her?

ABBIE. She's right, there's no going back. She should know there are compensations.

CONOR. You want me to do that?

ABBIE. Of course. She's our People. She's carried out a great act of courage, and she deserves our kindness.

WILLA. Ambassadors, I've spent many months among conversations I didn't understand; I don't think I care for another.

CONOR. Willa…

WILLA. Yes?

CONOR. May I touch different parts of your body to illustrate a point?

WILLA. Why do you need to ask?

(*Over the following,* CONOR *touches* WILLA.)

CONOR. Imagine something for me. Imagine yourself somehow separated from the Honeycomb and dragged into the atmosphere of a strange planet.

WILLA. How would that happen?

CONOR. Never mind how. It's not important. What's important is that the air is breathable, the vegetation edible, but the sound of the Honeycomb is drifting further and further away until you can't hear it anymore. What would you do then? Would you rage, pound the soil, destroy every object around you in your grief? Yes, of course you would – for a time. Until you exhausted yourself. And then, you would begin to look around yourself. At the trees, at the animals, at the sky. May I reach inside your shirt?

WILLA. Of course.

(CONOR *opens* WILLA*'s shirt and caresses her breasts.*)

CONOR. And having no other choice, you would study the trees, the animals, the sky. You would, having no alternative, begin to live with them. If you could find

a way, you would speak to them, and they to you. And
time would pass, and you would speak every day, and
the inevitable would follow.

WILLA. The inevitable?

CONOR. You would love them.

WILLA. Another metaphor.

CONOR. These weak, exposed bodies that feel everything:
they *feel everything*. Do you see? (*He removes his hands
from inside her shirt.*)

WILLA. Conor.

CONOR. Yes.

WILLA. Will you do it some more?

CONOR. Forgive me, I cannot.

WILLA. Why?

ABBIE. Sure you can.

CONOR. I only wanted to show you. I can't continue.

WILLA. Why not?

CONOR. I only go further with Abbie.

WILLA. But that doesn't make any sense.

ABBIE. Conor, I told you, I don't object.

CONOR. Why don't you object?

WILLA. Why would you only share a feeling like that with
one other?

CONOR. Abbie: why don't you object?

ABBIE. I learned from the Honeycomb: share everything.
The race I was born into, they say, "Let me make sure
I get everything I want and put it somewhere safe,
and once I've done that, I'll *think* about sharing." The
Honeycomb simply says: "Share. Nothing is mine. A
thing passed into my hands. Take it. May it make you as
happy as it made me."

CONOR. Forgive me. This was a mistake.

WILLA. Can I do it to myself?

ABBIE. You can. It's better with someone else.

WILLA. I won't have one of them touching me.

ABBIE. You won't have to. There'll be a lot more Transitioned People soon.

CONOR. But that's a waste!

WILLA. What is?

CONOR. Think of what we have. All the ones like you and me, all over the world. For twelve years now we haven't been able to build an understanding between our People and theirs. Why not?

WILLA. Because they refuse.

CONOR. Because we're too different! We have no basis for understanding each other! There's nothing we share – except for *us*. You and me. All the others like us. The halfway people. Think of it. What if we were to reveal ourselves?

WILLA. All the Transitioned People? Just announce ourselves?

CONOR. Yes! Think of it. We could be the connection. Transitioned People and humans, together. Bound by love and common skin, some even making and bringing up children, a *bridge race*. Able to reach in both directions, and build a real, lasting peace on this planet! Yes, we must never forget the cost, but we also should see the opportunity!

WILLA. What cost?

(**CONOR** *stares at her.*)

I don't understand what you mean by "cost."

CONOR. That every transition is the murder of a living consciousness. That cost.

WILLA. Abbie.

ABBIE. All right.

WILLA. This was your responsibility.

ABBIE. I was looking for the right time.

(**CONOR** *looks at both of them.*)

WILLA. It's too late. The responsibility's mine now.

CONOR. I'm beginning to believe that I keep the fewest secrets of anyone in this room.

ABBIE. You never go to the Honeycomb. If you spent more time in the Honeycomb you'd *know*.

WILLA. You said the Transitioned People will bring peace to this planet. You're right.

CONOR. I don't understand.

WILLA. A group is being assembled. Coral Farm will be the testing ground.

CONOR. A group of what?

WILLA. All volunteers. No one's being forced.

CONOR. Volunteers.

ABBIE. Sending Ronnie away isn't a solution. She'll just start again in Savannah.

WILLA. As soon as the number of volunteers equals the human population of Coral Farm, we'll begin taking humans into the Honeycomb in batches of one hundred.

CONOR. For what?

ABBIE. She smuggles people into this house every day for secret conferences. They won't let Willa listen. Seriously: what do you think that means?

WILLA. Why hunt for the explosives when we can simply remove the desire to use them?

ABBIE. At every farm in the world, they creep out at night, and they kill us. They've slapped away our open hands again and again. Haven't we tried hard enough?

CONOR. I would like one of you to tell me now that we are not discussing a mass transition of the Honeycomb into every human body on Coral Farm.

WILLA. Conor, you're not understanding me: Coral Farm *first. (silence)*

ABBIE. *(to WILLA)* I told you, I was looking for the right time.

CONOR. What would be the right time?

WILLA. Did you really think this wasn't being discussed?

CONOR. A mass murder? No, I didn't think so.

WILLA. Mass murder?

CONOR. They have a word for this.

ABBIE. Sweetheart, take a minute and think.

CONOR. They have a word for this, these people. Shall I teach it to you?

WILLA. *You're* Transitioned, Conor, do you think you're a murderer?

CONOR. Yes! I'm a murderer! I have the air on my skin and Abbie's body at night because I murdered a living soul and you call me by his name!

ABBIE. How does that make any sense?

WILLA. It doesn't. It makes no sense. You entered the body of a weak organism and improved it at tremendous cost to yourself.

CONOR. I made a bargain with these people! On behalf of the whole Honeycomb: Save our race and we'll save yours!

WILLA. We are saving this race! The only way we can! What would you prefer? To kill them? To let them kill us? Millions of us stand ready to give up our bodies so their bodies can live. Millions stand ready to give up the voice of the Honeycomb forever to save some *portion* of this wretched, awful race! I will not have you dishonor their sacrifice, dishonor *mine*, I will not have it!

ABBIE. Come home with me.

CONOR. I'll go to the Honeycomb.

ABBIE. That's right, that's where I'm going, too.

CONOR. I'll go to the Honeycomb and challenge the decision.

WILLA. Well, of course you can do that. *(beat)*

CONOR. But you already know they won't listen.

ABBIE. You've lost so much, baby. You lost your world, you lost so many centuries, floating through darkness, not knowing if you'd ever find a place to land. Don't you

think you deserve a little peace? Don't you deserve to
have a home?

WILLA. *(checking the window)* I think that's Ronnie and the
others. I'm not sure.

ABBIE. *(to* **CONOR***)* Let's go.

CONOR. Can I ask…

ABBIE. Let's just go now.

WILLA. Ask what?

CONOR. Could Abbie be spared?

ABBIE. Conor…

CONOR. He's done so much for us, surely, of anyone, Abbie
can be spared.

WILLA. What do you mean by "spared"?

ABBIE. I don't wanna be spared.

CONOR. I'm sure, I'm sure it's possible, I'll go before the
Queen, I'll put the question to the Honeycomb, after
all his service, surely his mind can be spared –

ABBIE. Conor: I don't want to be spared. I want to be *first.*

CONOR. But…

ABBIE. For my body? This weak body I've always hated, to
be home to one of the Honeycomb? I've wanted this
my whole life.

WILLA. *(looking out the window)* That's them, definitely.

CONOR. You won't know me anymore.

ABBIE. All the People of the Honeycomb know each other.
What do you mean?

WILLA. We don't want them to see us talking.

> *(She lies on the cot and pretends to be asleep.)*

CONOR. It won't be you.

ABBIE. It'll be better.

> **(SHIRLEY, RONNIE,** *and* **FEE** *enter through the
> front door.* **FEE** *and* **SHIRLEY** *carry buckets of
> water. All stop when they see* **ABBIE** *and* **CONOR***.)*

SHIRLEY. Ambassadors?

RONNIE. What are you doing here?

ABBIE. Came to see if you said your goodbyes.

RONNIE. Haven't had the baby yet.

SHIRLEY. *(to FEE)* Come on.

(They walk through with the water.)

ABBIE. Maybe give them some time to get used to the idea, maybe move your explosives to another location?

RONNIE. Great advice, bro! I'll think it over.

CONOR. I used to stand right here.

RONNIE. What?

CONOR. Late into the night. Watching the two of you talk. I didn't understand a word but I watched anyway.

RONNIE. *(headed up the stairs)* All right.

ABBIE. *(headed out the door)* We're leaving.

*(**CONOR**'s voice stops them.)*

CONOR. I was afraid to move. I was afraid to breathe. I thought the slightest sound would make you stop.

Ten

*(CLEM and DEV sit together as SHIRLEY passes
them bits of faded magazine. PECK sits by the door.)*

DEV. *(to CLEM)* Remember this?

CLEM. Yeah.

DEV. You had one, right?

CLEM. Not me personally, my parents.

SHIRLEY. It's called a laptop.

CLEM. Yeah, Shirley, I remember what it's called.

DEV. You could send somebody a message in another
farm – I guess not another farm –

SHIRLEY. Another city.

DEV. Another city, yeah! In, I don't know, like a second.
Remember?

(CLEM looks at him.)

What?

(RONNIE enters.)

RONNIE. Dev, Clem, I'm sorry to keep you guys sitting
around.

SHIRLEY. We're looking at pictures.

RONNIE. *(to CLEM.)* I just learned the last couple times, you
can't rush it when you're this far along. You have to sit
out there in the privy and just let it happen. Probably
don't need to tell you, right? What are we on?

DEV. Actually what's this?

RONNIE. Lemme see.

*(She studies the picture and then shows it to
SHIRLEY.)*

You know, Shirley, I'm gonna let you take this one – I
know you told me before –

SHIRLEY. It's 'cause you never had a job before the bugs,
that's what it is.

RONNIE. Guilty.

SHIRLEY. *(to* **DEV***)* It was a kind of phone. For businesses. You remember businesses, like companies?

DEV. Sure, of course.

SHIRLEY. You'd have this kind of phone in the middle of the table for when you talked to a lot of people at the same time. People in different places, all coming together to plan something over the phone.

RONNIE. What was that called, Shirley? When people did that?

CLEM. Oh, come on.

SHIRLEY. Conference call.

RONNIE. Conference call.

DEV. Conference call.

RONNIE. That was what she did every day, this woman. Talked to people from all over the world. Made plans with them. Created things in collaboration with them.

DEV. What things?

RONNIE. Pictures. Beautiful pictures to put in magazines so millions of people could see them.

CLEM. So, these are pictures…of a woman who makes pictures.

DEV. *(to* **CLEM***)* Look, we can just say no, we don't have to be like this.

CLEM. Like what?

RONNIE. My favorite picture, though, is on the other side.

DEV. *(turns the photo over)* Shit.

RONNIE. That's the same woman, and that's her mother with her.

DEV. She's really old!

RONNIE. Right here below the picture? It says she's eighty-two years old.

DEV. *(to* **CLEM***)* God, do you remember that? People used to live to eighty-two years.

CLEM. Oh, Dev, fucking stop.

DEV. What?

CLEM. You're walking right into it.

DEV. Into what?

CLEM. "Remember, Dev? Remember how people used to live to eighty-two years? Remember how before the bugs came, there was all this magic medicine, so magic that everyone who took it lived to be eighty-two years old? Wouldn't you love your little baby girl to live eighty-two years? All you have to do is drink bugwater and die!"

DEV. We can just say no.

RONNIE. Clem, I know how you feel, the only reason – *(Over the following she cues* **SHIRLEY**.*)*

CLEM. You know how I feel? Well sure, you know how I feel, we have so much in common. We've both had babies. We both remember how right near the end you can't hardly shit right. It's like we're the same person! I guess I should drink bugwater and die.

RONNIE. All right, you know what? Fuck this. I'm not listening to this, not one more second. You can't show any respect for me?

CLEM. What is this respect shit?

RONNIE. Then you can get out!

CLEM. No one can answer me: Respect fucking *what?*

DEV. All right, all right, we're leaving.

RONNIE. That's right, you're leaving, get the fuck out!

SHIRLEY. That's enough, Ronnie!

CLEM. Really? Get out? 'Cause we'll do that. We'll be *happy* to do that.

DEV. Let's just go.

RONNIE. *(grabs* **CLEM** *by the arm.)* Let me show you the way!

DEV. Ronnie, seriously, let go of her –

SHIRLEY. Okay that is enough of this SHIT!

       (She pulls **RONNIE** *off of* **CLEM** *and shoves her.)*

   Are you off your mind?

RONNIE. She can't keep her stupid mouth shut!

SHIRLEY. Clem is my guest in this house, Dev is my guest in this house. Are you a savage?

RONNIE. I'm just sick of –

SHIRLEY. Sit down. Sit the fuck down and do not talk until I say. Ask yourself if I'm joking.

(**RONNIE** *sits down.*)

I'm sorry, Clem, Dev, I'm really sorry. You can go.

DEV. We can go?

CLEM. We could always go.

SHIRLEY. Thank you for hearing us out. I'm sorry, you deserved better from this house.

CLEM. *(to* **DEV***)* Well come on.

DEV. Shirley – Ronnie...you've gotta understand, we have it pretty good.

SHIRLEY. You don't have to explain anything.

DEV. You know, we've got good work details...the Nampas treat us okay...

CLEM. Dev: why would she want to hear this?

DEV. Well, I'm just – we don't want to mess with it, okay?

SHIRLEY. We understand.

DEV. We're able to see each other a lot, we sneak out no problem... We get to see Shayla at House One like every other day, the Nampas just wave us right in.

SHIRLEY. You don't have to explain anything to us, Dev. You're free people. Well you're not free people, but in *our* eyes you are.

CLEM. That's really nice, Shirley. That's pretty. Can I ask you a question?

SHIRLEY. What?

DEV. Why don't we just go?

CLEM. Are you faking?

SHIRLEY. Excuse me?

CLEM. 'Cause you know how much I hate Ronnie, right? And if you know that, you know much I love seeing Ronnie put in her place. So what I'm saying is, did you really get mad at Ronnie just now, or did you fake it to make it seem like you're on my side against her, to make me and Dev feel grateful to you, so we'll drink bugwater and die?

(**SHIRLEY** *looks at* **RONNIE**.)

CLEM. Why are you looking at Ronnie? Does Ronnie know the answer?

SHIRLEY. *(to* **RONNIE***)* I mean…

RONNIE. It's okay, forget it.

SHIRLEY. Yep.

CLEM. What did you think, people leave here and they never talk about it again? You think I'm so stupid I don't ask questions about a house before I walk into it?

RONNIE. But you still haven't left.

CLEM. We are leaving.

RONNIE. You're being smart, Clem, but you're not being smart enough. Figure out what's bothering you.

DEV. We're leaving. All right? We're leaving.

CLEM. I know what's bothering me.

RONNIE. You're the type of person who puts details together. We wouldn't have figured out about the bugwater if you weren't. Put the details together now.

DEV. Come on, Clem.

RONNIE. How is it you know all my moves before I can make them?

CLEM. I told you, I asked around.

RONNIE. How many people did you talk to?

CLEM. A lot of people.

RONNIE. And how were there a lot of people for you to talk to?

CLEM. 'Cause you've half the goddam farm in here!

RONNIE. Half the goddam farm. Folks who said yes, folks who said no. For six months now. Now do you wanna finish this thought or should I?

DEV. Or neither, okay? Let's say neither.

CLEM. How close are you?

RONNIE. Forty-eight. Three more and we go. *(beat)* Now what's strange is you and me were carrying together in this house for months. And you may not like me, but you keep your mouth shut. And your man's loyal all the way. So how is it I spent six months going all the way up to forty-eight, and I'm only just talking to you now?

(**RONNIE** *pushes the photo into* **CLEM**'s *hands.*)

Take another look at her: making her pictures, talking to her people all over the world, her mind racing every minute of the day.

People say, "What about Clem? Let's try Clem," and I say "No fucking way, and here's why: Clem's bored. I mean soul-deep *bored.* Clem's got a brain in her bigger and faster than any flyer you've ever seen. Connections and plans are happening in there all the time. She wants to turn that brain to things, she wants to build things, she wants to command whole teams of people to make amazing things…but she can't. So that big brain's eating itself alive. There's gonna be a world after the bugs, and that world *needs that big restless brain inside Clem.*" That's how desperate I am, that I'm breaking my biggest rule: We don't use Clem. It kills me to come to you like this.

DEV. You didn't come to me either.

RONNIE. Well, Dev, I know I couldn't face the war that's coming without my man, and I couldn't ask her to, either. I hope you don't feel put down.

DEV. No. I don't.

CLEM. Really? You don't? You really should.

DEV. *(to* **RONNIE***)* Don't miss much, do you?

RONNIE. I look really hard at the people I love. I bet you do too, right?

CLEM. Right about what?

DEV. I try to think of things to talk to you about, but anything I can think of you thought of a long time ago.

CLEM. Don't let her do that to you, that's not true!

DEV. It's not? What does it mean when you go quiet for so long and nothing I say can bring you out?

CLEM. Don't ask me this in front of her!

DEV. *(holding up the magazine)* If there was a man out there like this woman – think about it now, think about it – would you be with him or would you be with me?

CLEM. This is some shit Ronnie's doing to you, Dev, this is all about her!

DEV. Well, I guess that works for an answer.

CLEM. Dev, Dev, *Dev*. it's not like that. You *know* I love you.

DEV. Yeah, I know, but…you love me *anyway*, right? *(beat)*

CLEM. But I do love you.

DEV. See? I get it. *(They hold each other.)*

CLEM. *(to* **RONNIE***)* Fuck you. *Fuck you.*

RONNIE. If your little Shayla takes after Dev, she'll be all right. Not great, she won't live eighty-two years, but she'll be fine. But if she takes after *you*…well, you tell me. I wouldn't presume to tell you.

CLEM. Why not you?

RONNIE. What's that?

CLEM. Why not you instead of me? If I'm this great thinker we're gonna need later, why not you and Peck instead of Dev and me? 'Cause all *you* look like to me? Is the cold-blooded murdering daughter of the man who put us here in the first place.

RONNIE. I could do that. Of course I could. And I will, if you want. Only one thing: if I take your place you have to take mine.

CLEM. What does that mean?

RONNIE. I need at least one more. And that's just for this time. I'll need a whole lot more after that. I can walk into the Honeycomb with a bottle of bugwater, but then you have to get the volunteers for next time. You have to live today all over again, but on the other side, asking people for the worst thing anyone can ask for. How does that sound? I am the daughter of the man who put us here. You're absolutely right. But you know what that is? That's your guarantee. That's how you know I'll never stop.

> *(Pounding on the front door.* **PECK**, **SHIRLEY** *and* **RONNIE** *tense up, go for reapers.)*

CONOR. *(offstage)* Ronnie! You have to let me in!

RONNIE. Get them out of here.

SHIRLEY. This way.

> *(**SHIRLEY** hurries **CLEM** and **DEV** into the kitchen. **RONNIE** motions **PECK** to the window.)*

CONOR. Ronnie? Please let me in. I'm alone. I took a boat. I'm completely alone.

> *(**PECK**, at the window, nods to **RONNIE**. She opens the door and **CONOR** rushes in.)*

RONNIE. Skin?

CONOR. Listen to me: how are you causing the explosions?

RONNIE. You tell me.

CONOR. There's no *time* for this!

PECK. *(advancing with reaper)* Easy now.

CONOR. All right. All right.

RONNIE. Let's try this again.

CONOR. Where is Willa right now?

RONNIE. Upstairs with Fee. Why do you care?

CONOR. I'm not the only Transitioned person in the world. It's a lie. I'm not the only Skin.

> *(**RONNIE** takes that in.)*

RONNIE. *(to **PECK**)* Tell Fee! Go!

> *(**PECK** hurries upstairs as quietly as he can.)*

CONOR. I could be killed for what I'm about to tell you.

RONNIE. Then you better get started.

Eleven

(**CONOR**, **RONNIE**, **SHIRLEY** *and* **PECK**.)

CONOR. It makes sense.

RONNIE. It does?

CONOR. Our fertilization cycle restarts roughly every twelve of your years. Our bodies change as it approaches, so the glandular runoff we release during pollination becomes more...

RONNIE. Potent?

SHIRLEY. The smell.

CONOR. If the runoff had to reach a certain concentration level to...trigger the reaction it would explain why it's never happened before. It's only a theory, of course.

SHIRLEY. You know we can't let you walk out of here. What you told us, what we told you.

PECK. But if anybody's gonna be missed...

RONNIE. Fuck.

CONOR. I won't betray you.

RONNIE. Yeah, thanks for that. You and my father betrayed *my* race and now you're here betraying *your* race, but you won't betray *us*.

CONOR. Correct. *(beat)*

RONNIE. You know the plan, now. Tell us what'll happen.

CONOR. If you succeed.

RONNIE. I know what'll happen if we fail.

CONOR. I can't be certain.

RONNIE. You never saw a nest fall before?

CONOR. Not myself. But the Honeycomb holds the memory.

RONNIE. And?

CONOR. Chaos. The Queen was killed on impact. The telepathic net shattered. Imagine a blinding light in your eyes while hundreds of voices scream in your ears. Until a few of the People – essentially working blind – rebuilt a portion of the Honeycomb, the rest of the hive was incapacitated to the point of catatonia.

SHIRLEY. Ronnie, holy shit, this could be –

RONNIE. Wait. *(to CONOR)* Our goal was: take the nest down, make you afraid, prove to our people it works, and use that proof to get more volunteers. But it could be more, right?

CONOR. It could be a great deal more.

RONNIE. There's a window of time...after the Honeycomb falls but before they start rebuilding...

CONOR. And if you can...neutralize the rebuilders, the time window expands. And as long as the Honeycomb is in chaos...

RONNIE. They can't warn other hives.

CONOR. Correct.

SHIRLEY. *Ronnie.*

RONNIE. Yeah.

PECK. *(gesturing at CONOR)* Assuming...

RONNIE. Yeah. *(to CONOR)* Why would you tell us this?

CONOR. Because you're out of time. They're coming for you. They'll start rounding you up for mass transitions in the morning.

SHIRLEY. *Tomorrow* morning?

RONNIE. I thought you said they needed volunteers.

CONOR. They have them.

SHIRLEY. Enough for the whole farm? Seven thousand heads?

CONOR. They have the volunteers.

RONNIE. When did they start asking?

CONOR. Five days ago.

> *(RONNIE, PECK, and SHIRLEY look at each other.)*

RONNIE. Well shit, that's one for you guys, it's taken us six months to get to fifty!

WILLA. *(offstage)* But I've been up here for two days!

RONNIE. *(to* CONOR*)* Be ready to leave.

CONOR. They're coming for you at first light. You have to act *now*.

RONNIE. So here's what I'm wondering: Why the fuck do you care?

CONOR. You asked what happened when the Honeycomb fell. You didn't ask *why* it fell.

RONNIE. Pretend I did.

CONOR. We did it. Our own carelessness. We horribly misused our planet and then were shocked when it cracked open beneath our feet. So I know that can happen. I've seen it. When I made the agreement with your father, I believed – I *still* believe – I was sparing your people the same fate.

RONNIE. At the cost of billions of lives.

CONOR. Yes. Horrific. But for an honorable result. But this…to colonize every human mind, to overwrite the consciousness of an entire race… The People of the Honeycomb are not just our bodies; we are *thoughts*, we are *memories*, we are a *story*. And yet we would steal these very treasures from you, and leave only your bodies behind. Your language has many words for many purposes, but for this purpose there is only one.

RONNIE. Yeah, I see that.

CONOR. Thank you.

RONNIE. It's strange that I still don't believe it.

CONOR. It's Abbie. *(beat)*

RONNIE. Keep talking.

CONOR. He won't be Abbie anymore.

RONNIE. Abbie doesn't get a pass?

CONOR. He's asked to be first.

RONNIE. He's…

CONOR. I'm sorry.

SHIRLEY. Jesus Christ.

*(*RONNIE *absorbs it.* PECK *goes to her.)*

RONNIE. You know there was a time…

PECK. Easy.

RONNIE. There was a time I would've murdered for him. Anyone. Just point them out.

CONOR. I'm murdering for him now. *(beat)* How many more do you need?

(**RONNIE** *looks at* **SHIRLEY**.)

SHIRLEY. They're in.

RONNIE. *(to* **CONOR***)* One.

PECK. *(to* **RONNIE***)* We should step upstairs.

RONNIE. I don't look busy?

PECK. Or we can talk in front of them.

RONNIE. Fuck you.

PECK. You heard what the man said, Ron, we have to go *now*!

RONNIE. You think I can't find one?

PECK. Tonight? Right now? Tell me who!

CONOR. I could be persuaded to take the honor.

(They all look at him.)

RONNIE. Why?

CONOR. The Honeycomb won't forgive me. Abbie won't forgive me. Nowhere left I can call home. I will take the honor under two conditions.

RONNIE. Go.

CONOR. If you're victorious you'll spare my people. Let them have part of the planet.

RONNIE. Can't.

CONOR. Then let them leave to find another.

RONNIE. You won't be here to know if I kept my end.

CONOR. Ronnie, I watched you grow up. I know who and what you are.

RONNIE. The other?

CONOR. Abbie. Make sure he always has a home with you. *(beat)*

RONNIE. Yeah.

SHIRLEY. Shit, Ronnie, he's in the Honeycomb all the time. If we hit it, nine out of ten he's there.

CONOR. You have to make sure he's not! Ronnie, we have a deal, you have to make sure he's not!

RONNIE. That's on you, Conor! He's not gonna do anything I say!

CONOR. If I tell him –

RONNIE. You can't.

CONOR. I can't lie to him!

RONNIE. Sure you can. You're one of us now.

CONOR. But… I've always felt…

RONNIE. What?

CONOR. Two humans…that love each other…that's like a Honeycomb. A place without lies.

RONNIE. No. We're not like that. We can lie to people we love. That's what you're gonna do now.

CONOR. How?

RONNIE. You don't go home, he'll come looking for you here.

CONOR. How do I lie to him?

RONNIE. I'll help you.

FEE. *(from upstairs)* It's not problem, we can bring up anything you need!

RONNIE. Fuck!

PECK. I can stash him at Kel's.

RONNIE. Do it. And Peck: Get the word out. *Get everybody ready.*

PECK. Yeah. *(to* **CONOR***)* Come on.

> *(He pushes* **CONOR** *through the kitchen door. To* **RONNIE***:)*

Don't move on her 'til I'm back. I'm not kidding.

RONNIE. She's as big as me, she's not gonna do shit.

PECK. Neither will you. *(He exits after* **CONOR***.)*

WILLA. *(just behind the stairs)* I can't, please, I just can't!

    *(**WILLA** enters with **FEE** behind her.)*

I'm sorry, Ronnie, Shirley, I don't mean to listen to your conversation, I just can't be up there anymore.

SHIRLEY. That's fine!

WILLA. I need to go outside, I need to be around people.

FEE. I'm people.

RONNIE. That's fine, Willa.

    (Splashes outside; people running away.)

WILLA. *(moving toward a window)* Oh, was someone here?

    *(**RONNIE** intercepts her.)*

RONNIE. Why do you ask?

SHIRLEY. Willa, we'd love to hang out with you downstairs.

RONNIE. *(gesturing to the couch)* Why don't you sit down? I'll bet your ankles are the size of a house.

WILLA. That's not necessary, Ronnie, you can sit down, you need it more than me.

RONNIE. It's big enough for both of us. We could both sit down.

    (Neither one sits down.)

SHIRLEY. I got veggies left over. Anybody hungry?

WILLA. I just couldn't be up in that room anymore.

RONNIE. Willa, I've got eyes. I can guess what it's been like for you in this house. Losing your memory, having to start all over again, then us shooing you out of the room all the time, plus the baby through all of it...

WILLA. I understand that you have to be careful.

RONNIE. That's right, we have to be careful.

WILLA. I respect that, I just –

RONNIE. But not anymore.

WILLA. What?

RONNIE. You've done your time. You've proved you can keep your mouth shut, you've proved you can pull your weight. The freezeout ends today.

SHIRLEY. Welcome downstairs, kid.

  *(**WILLA** stares at them for a beat.)*

WILLA. Thank you, Ronnie.

RONNIE. Hey. C'mere.

  (They hug as best as they can.)

RONNIE. You earned it.

  (They separate.)

Well hell, Shirley, what about those veggies?

  *(Over the following, **WILLA** quietly picks up a reaper.)*

SHIRLEY. I thought you were still hugging.

RONNIE. *(heading for the back)* Tell you what, I'll start the firepot, get the water boiling, you take a look at what we –

FEE. Shirley!

  *(**WILLA** stabs **SHIRLEY**. **RONNIE** turns at **SHIRLEY**'s cry. Tries to get a reaper of her own. **WILLA** frees her reaper and swings it at **RONNIE**.)*

RONNIE. *(to **FEE**)* Get Peck! He's headed for Kel's, get him back!

  *(**FEE** flees. **WILLA** comes after **RONNIE**, swinging her reaper.)*

  *(The fight is awful. Both women are fighters – **WILLA** is meticulous, **RONNIE** is ferocious – but both are badly balanced, sore, and trying to protect their bellies at the same time. It's ugly, inelegant, and bruising. **WILLA** is better trained, and nearly bests **RONNIE**, but **RONNIE**'s hatred and rage win out. She gets **WILLA** on her back as she approaches her, reaper in hand.)*

WILLA. Ronnie…all right… Ronnie…wait…the baby…the baby, my baby, my baby, Ronnie, MY BABY!

RONNIE. You don't mean it.

> **(RONNIE** *brings the reaper down. She watches* **WILLA** *die.* **PECK** *and* **FEE** *enter.)*

PECK. Jesus Fuck! *(He runs to* **RONNIE**.*)*

RONNIE. Get me to her.

PECK. Shut up. *(He examines her.)*

RONNIE. Banged up, that's all. Get me to her.

> **(PECK** *helps* **RONNIE** *get to* **SHIRLEY**'s *body.)*

Here, here.

> *(She kneels by* **SHIRLEY** *and tries to pull her up.)*

PECK. I got it.

> *(He raises* **SHIRLEY**'s *upper body so* **RONNIE** *can pull her into an embrace.* **RONNIE** *rocks* **SHIRLEY** *in her arms.)*

FEE. *(finding* **WILLA**'s *body)* Oh shit, oh shit, look at this.

PECK. Ron – listen –

RONNIE. MOTHERFUCKER!

PECK. All right. All right.

FEE. The baby…

RONNIE. She gave me everything. Like I deserved it.

PECK. All right, you have to suck that in now.

RONNIE. Like I deserved it just 'cause she gave it to me.

PECK. You gotta suck that inside.

RONNIE. No.

PECK. Suck it inside and save it for later 'cause you gotta put her down and we gotta talk now.

RONNIE. Fuck you!

PECK. You know we do. Shirley was one.

> *(A horrible beat.)*

RONNIE. Fee?

FEE. Yeah?

RONNIE. Come over here, Fee.

> (FEE *crosses to* RONNIE.)

PECK. Ron, what are you doing?

RONNIE. Fee, you see Shirley dead here?

FEE. Yeah, Ronnie.

RONNIE. You know all she did for us, all she was going to do for us?

FEE. Yeah, Ronnie.

RONNIE. *(holds up her bloody hands)* What is this? Tell me what this is.

FEE. Shirley's blood.

PECK. Ronnie, come on.

RONNIE. You gotta do the right thing now, Fee.

FEE. Ronnie, I'm... I'm *carrying.*

RONNIE. You gotta do the right thing, Fee! You gotta do the right thing by her *body*! You gotta do the right thing by *her blood on this floor!!*

> (PECK *slaps* RONNIE *in the face. She stares at him.)*

PECK. Get out of here, Fee. Make sure everyone's ready to move. Who's gonna be here before?

FEE. Um...

PECK. Fee!

FEE. Me n' Jimmy. Clem n' Dev.

PECK. Find them, then get them back here at the time we talked about. Go! (FEE *runs out.)*

RONNIE. Forgive me.

PECK. Every baby. You say it every single day. We need every baby.

RONNIE. It can't be you.

PECK. Who? In the time we have left?

RONNIE. We'll get, we'll get...

PECK. Seriously. 'Cause I don't wanna do it. Who? *(pause)*

RONNIE. Me.

PECK. What?

RONNIE. Me instead of you.

PECK. *(meaning her belly)* What's this?

RONNIE. I don't even want it!

PECK. We're not talking about it.

RONNIE. Oh, oh, because they "need me."

PECK. Don't goddamn say it like that, it's true!

RONNIE. Well if they need me they need you 'cause I can't live without you.

PECK. Fuck that.

RONNIE. I can't live without you.

PECK. There's our babies. There's all the people that count on you. There's a hundred million bugs to throw belly-up on the campfire. You can. Because you have to.

RONNIE. When you're not in the bed I don't sleep.

PECK. Then you'll learn.

RONNIE. I barely had you.

PECK. What're you talking about?

RONNIE. We're always apart, we're always running, I've barely had you at ALL!

PECK. What "barely," you have all of me. Just all of me.

(*They kiss and embrace.*)

I have to go get Conor back.

RONNIE. Take me upstairs first.

PECK. We have enough time?

RONNIE. Whatever's enough. Whatever there is, is enough. Nothing's enough so I'll take anything.

Twelve

(Late night, nearing dawn. **CONOR** *sits on the couch looking through the box of* **ABBIE**'s *drawings.* **ABBIE** *enters.)*

ABBIE. Conor?

CONOR. They're all asleep. Willa as well.

ABBIE. Have you been here all this time?

CONOR. *(meaning the box)* Did you know about this?

ABBIE. Sure.

CONOR. You weren't afraid they would be lost?

ABBIE. I didn't care. I don't care *now.* Put it out with the kindling.

CONOR. Truly?

ABBIE. Of all things, we're gonna wring our hands over this?

CONOR. Look at this one.

*(***CONOR*** *gives him a drawing.* ***ABBIE*** *studies it.)*

ABBIE. Huh. Raf.

CONOR. There is no human Honeycomb. You can't share thoughts so you have to look at faces. I used to think, "How savage. How insane." But there's something in contemplation. I didn't see it for a long time.

ABBIE. I'm sorry I didn't tell you about the contingency. I was working up the courage. That's the truth.

CONOR. I think I could stare at human faces for a thousand years and never grow tired.

ABBIE. Yeah, I thought that too.

CONOR. It's not true?

ABBIE. Just when you're thinking it's the bottomless mystery you smack into the bottom. "When can I sleep?" "When can I eat?" "*What* can I eat?" "When can I get drunk?" "When can I jerk off?" "When will someone love me?" "When will the people who love me leave me alone?" Face after face after face, and what did they need more than anything?

CONOR. I don't know.

ABBIE. A goddam alien invasion. *(beat)*

CONOR. I only thought…the mind that made these…is worth mourning.

ABBIE. The Honeycomb doesn't mourn. "There's too much that's living to think of the dead."

CONOR. Yes.

ABBIE. Your words.

CONOR. Yes, thank you.

ABBIE. I'll go to the Honeycomb in the morning for the transition. One of the People will be waiting for me there. Then the telepathic link: one mind will perish, one body will perish, but a new creature will be born. A child, imbued with the wisdom of ten thousand years, but still a child, and we'll need someone to take care of us. *(indicating* CONOR*)* So we'll have the best caretaker in the world. We won't know how to eat so you'll teach us how. We won't know how to walk so you'll teach us how. We won't know the language so we'll learn from the living master. And we'll be shivering inside our soft, prickling skin, and it'll be you that teaches us not to be afraid. The same skin that's always welcomed your touch. The same body that's always been yours. You get to teach us that same happiness you taught me, all over again. When does that ever happen? Who ever gets that privilege? There's too much that's living to think of the dead.

CONOR. I'm sure that you're right.

ABBIE. I promise I won't keep secrets from you anymore.

CONOR. In the morning, then?

ABBIE. Just after sunrise. Along with a few hundred others.

CONOR. Will you do something for me?

ABBIE. Of course.

CONOR. Do you remember where we used to go?

ABBIE. When?

CONOR. Just after, but before the Honeycomb was finished.

ABBIE. You mean east? The dry stretch?

CONOR. Under the old road.

ABBIE. Of course I remember.

CONOR. Will you wait for me there?

ABBIE. You mean now?

CONOR. You won't remember the place tomorrow, will you?

ABBIE. What's wrong?

CONOR. Will you go there, now, and wait for me? I may need an hour.

ABBIE. Conor...you know how many duties I –

CONOR. This is the last thing I can ever ask of you. Will you do it or not?

ABBIE. Yes, of course.

CONOR. I may need an hour. Please wait for me. Lie on the dry patch, under the old road, where we used to go, and wait for me.

ABBIE. I will.

> (CONOR *kisses* ABBIE *and holds him tight.*)

You understand, this isn't an end, this is a beginning –

CONOR. *Now.* Go now. Please.

> (ABBIE *leaves through the front door.*)

All right.

> (RONNIE *emerges from the kitchen.*)

You know where to find him.

RONNIE. We'll bring him in.

CONOR. And keep him safe?

RONNIE. And keep him safe. You need a minute?

CONOR. No. Let them come.

> (RONNIE *carries a lamp to a window and covers and then uncovers it. She repeats this at different windows.* CONOR *shows her the romance novel.*)

CONOR. This passage here. I marked it with berry juice. Of course you will not say "Douglas" or "Anna," you'll use the real names.

RONNIE. I got it.

(**PECK** *enters.*)

PECK. We're good.

RONNIE. You talked to the teams? They know to come here first?

PECK. They know.

RONNIE. If anyone moves before the Honeycomb falls –

PECK. They know.

RONNIE. Peck…

PECK. Will you marry me?

RONNIE. Fuck you.

(**FEE** *enters with* **JIMMY**.)

FEE. We're ready.

RONNIE. Bottles.

FEE. Yeah.

(**FEE** *exits up the stairs.*)

JIMMY. Not like totally sure what we're doing, so…

PECK. They'll tell you. It's easy.

(**CLEM** *and* **DEV** *enter.*)

DEV. Ready for us?

JIMMY. My brother! I didn't you know you guys were gonna be up in here!

DEV. Yeah.

JIMMY. Back to*gether*!

DEV. It's nice to see you, Jimmy.

CLEM. *(to* **RONNIE***)* You know which one she is?

RONNIE. Yeah.

CLEM. You do? Shayla? Really?

RONNIE. No, I don't know which one she is, but I'll put all bodies including mine in front of any baby. You don't have to like me to know I'll do that.

CLEM. That'll have to do.

(**FEE** *comes down the stairs with a covered basket.*)

FEE. Ronnie.

RONNIE. Five?

FEE. Five.

RONNIE. Okay, the bottles are in the bag, nobody leaves without getting a bottle from the bag.

JIMMY. Oh yeah! Boom time!

(*He shoves* **DEV** *playfully.*)

You know what I'm saying?

RONNIE. *(to* **FEE***)* Ready?

FEE. *(to* **JIMMY***)* Stand over here, baby. Hold my hand.

RONNIE. In the time before, someone always stood where I'm standing now and said something about what this promise means. Something nice, sometimes something beautiful. Because they had the time. But we don't, and neither do any of the people doing this in all the houses around us right now. So instead, I'm gonna give you *my* promise: I won't waste this. One day your children will tell their children, "We live free because of what began that day," and then they'll list your names, all of your names, because they'll know them by heart. They'll tear me to pieces before that isn't true. *(to* **FEE** *and* **JIMMY***)* Ready?

FEE. *(to* **JIMMY***)* Just say "I do" when she asks you.

JIMMY. On it, on it.

RONNIE. Do you, Fiona, take James to be your husband, to have and to hold from this day forward…

JIMMY. James?

(**FEE** *gives him a look.*)

Oh right!

RONNIE. ...for better or worse, for richer or poorer, in sickness and in health, to love and honor all the days of your life?

FEE. I do.

JIMMY. That's *right!*

RONNIE. Do you, James, take Fiona to be your wife, to have and to hold from this day forward, for better or worse, for richer or poorer, in sickness and in health, to love and honor all the days of your life?

JIMMY. This is...

(*She nods.*)

I *do!* Right?

RONNIE. I pronounce you husband and wife. You may kiss to seal your union.

JIMMY. We uh...

FEE. Kiss me.

(*They kiss.*)

RONNIE. (*to* **CLEM** *and* **DEV**) Okay?

JIMMY. (*to* **DEV**) You're up, brother! Do it right!

RONNIE. Do you, Clementine, take Devan to be your husband, to have and to hold from this day forward, for better or worse, for richer or poorer, in sickness and in health, to love and honor all the days of your life?

CLEM. I do.

RONNIE. Do you, Devan, take Clementine to be your wife, to have and to hold from this day forward, for better or worse, for richer or poorer, in sickness and in health, to love and honor all the days of your life?

DEV. I do.

JIMMY. That's my *boy!*

FEE. Ssh, baby.

RONNIE. I pronounce you man and wife. You may kiss to seal your union.

CLEM. Your beautiful eyes.

DEV. I love you. I love you.

(*They kiss.* **RONNIE** *turns to* **PECK**.)

RONNIE. So… I guess what we'll do is…

PECK. Anything's fine.

RONNIE. If I read first, and you –

CONOR. May I? (*He puts his hand out for the book.*)

RONNIE. Are you sure?

(**CONOR** *takes the book from her.*)

CONOR. I know your formal name is Veronica, and…?

RONNIE. (*indicating* **PECK**) Randall. Can you believe it?

PECK. Nah, fuck Randall. I was Peck before the bugs. It's all anyone's ever called me.

CONOR. Peck, then.

RONNIE. (*to* **CONOR**) Ronnie, then. (*beat*) I'm sorry.

CONOR. What are you sorry for?

RONNIE. That your own isn't here tonight. That I'm not doing this for you.

PECK. (*to* **RONNIE**) C'mere.

(*He holds her.* **CONOR** *finds the place in the book.*)

CONOR. Do you, Ronnie, take Peck to be your husband, to have and to hold from this day forward, for better or worse, for richer or poorer, in sickness and in health, to love and honor all the days of your life?

RONNIE. I do.

CONOR. Do you, Peck, take Ronnie to be your wife, to have and to hold from this day forward, for better or worse, for richer or poorer, in sickness and in health, to love and honor all the days of your life?

PECK. I do.

CONOR. I pronounce you man and wife. You may kiss to seal your union.

(**RONNIE** *and* **PECK** *kiss, intensely.* **PECK** *breaks it off first.*)

PECK. We have to move. Everybody get a bottle.

RONNIE. Fee.

(**FEE** *passes out bottles to* **JIMMY, CLEM, DEV, PECK,** *and* **CONOR.**)

PECK. Everybody remembers positions? Jimmy?

JIMMY. What's "Jimmy"? I got it.

PECK. We're moving out.

FEE. *(to* **JIMMY***)* You gotta go.

JIMMY. Wait, you're not…

PECK. She's carrying. This is as far as she goes.

JIMMY. I knew that. I knew that.

RONNIE. Clem.

(**CLEM** *walks past* **RONNIE** *without looking at her.*)

DEV. Goodbye, Ronnie.

CLEM. Let's go.

DEV. Jimmy.

(**JIMMY** *and* **FEE** *are kissing.*)

Jimmy.

JIMMY. That's the look. Right there.

(*He follows* **DEV** *and* **CLEM** *to the door as they exit, and then turns back to* **FEE.***)*\

Oh shit, I just, I just –

DEV. Jimmy. *(He grabs* **JIMMY** *and pulls him out the door.)*

RONNIE. Conor?

CONOR. I love this house. I lived for centuries before I came here, but this house…

PECK. You up for this?

CONOR. When my People look at their lives, they ask the question: "What small thing did I do to build the Honeycomb?"

RONNIE. What's your answer?

CONOR. I built the Honeycomb by saving its honor. Remember what you promised me.

RONNIE. I don't forget my promises. I'd be honored to call you my brother.

CONOR. You have a brother. *(He leaves.)*

RONNIE. Oh, fuck. Oh, my god.

PECK. This window right here?

> *(RONNIE holds PECK and buries her face in his chest.)*

Should be able to see it from this window. When I'm drinking? I'm gonna picture you here at this window.

RONNIE. I could eat the flesh right off your body.

PECK. Do it.

> *(RONNIE bites into PECK's chest. He holds her. Then he breaks away and walks out the front door without looking back. When she's able to, RONNIE goes to the window and watches. FEE approaches her.)*

FEE. Ronnie?

> *(She reaches a hand out to touch her. RONNIE's voice makes her pull her hand back.)*

RONNIE. You know where the first two teams are waiting?

FEE. Yeah. They're ready for you.

RONNIE. Get them, and get them in here.

FEE. Okay, Ronnie.

RONNIE. *Now.*

FEE. What did Skin mean? What did you promise him?

RONNIE. If we win I let the bugs leave to find another home.

FEE. We're gonna do that?

RONNIE. No we're not gonna that. We're gonna kill them, and we're not gonna stop killing them until we kill them all. Now do what I said and get the first two teams in here now.

(**FEE** *hurries out the front door.* **RONNIE** *turns to the window. She watches.*)

(*Lights down.*)

End of Play